Camp Club Girls

Sydney's D.C. Discovery

Published by Barbour Publishing, Inc., P.O. Box 719, Uhrichsville, Ohio 44683, www.barbourbooks.com

Our mission is to publish and distribute inspirational products offering exceptional value and biblical encouragement to the masses.

Member of the
Evangelical Christian
Publishers Association

Printed in the United States of America.

Dickinson Press Inc., Grand Rapids, MI. Job # 36503 11/13/09

Camp Club Girls
Sydney's D.C. Discovery

Jean Fischer

BARBOUR
PUBLISHING

Go 64

Splaaaashhh! Whoosh!

"Watch out!" someone called near Sydney's ear.

But it was too late. The pent-up explosion of the water landed square against Sydney's back, knocking her to the ground.

Dazed, she rolled onto her back and looked up into the hot summer sky. The water swirled around her whole body. From a distance she heard happy shouting and water gushing onto the street.

A fireman's face appeared above her. "Are you okay, little girl?"

Little girl? Little girl! I'm twelve years old! I'm not a little girl, mister.

The indignation snapped Sydney out of her dazed condition. She looked up and saw that two firemen were now looking at her anxiously. Carefully they helped her to her feet.

"Are you okay, little girl?"

She looked in the fireman's face. He seemed so worried that her irritation melted.

Sydney looked down at her soaked gray tank top and shorts. "Yes, sir, I'm fine," she said. "Thank you," she added, remembering her manners.

Sydney Lincoln had been talking to one of her neighborhood friends. She hadn't even noticed the firemen at the fire hydrant behind her. And she sure hadn't realized she was in the direct line of the nozzle the men were releasing.

Still out of breath from the shock of the water, Sydney dropped onto the curb in front of her house. She tore off her running shoes and socks and stuck her bare feet into the gutter. She watched as the water from the hydrant down the street shot into the air and out the nozzle. The neighborhood kids laughed and splashed in its flow.

As Sydney's clothes began to dry in the torrid sun, the water rushed along the curb like a river. It streamed between Sydney's toes and sent goose bumps creeping up to her knees.

Sydney lived in the middle of a row of brick houses. The two-story houses were connected so they looked like one long building. The only windows were in the front and the back. The houses were close to the street, and each had a narrow front porch with three steps leading to a tiny front yard and the sidewalk.

The screen door on Sydney's house swung open, and her mom stepped outside. "Sydney, have you seen your aunt Dee yet?" Her curly black hair was pulled back with a blue band to keep it off of her face.

"No, Mom," Sydney answered. "I ran past the Metro station looking for her, but she wasn't there."

"Well, when she gets here, you two come inside. Dinner's ready."

Sydney dipped her fingers into the water and splashed some onto her long, thin arms.

"Don't you want to come in by the air-conditioning?" Her mother fanned herself with a magazine. "Aren't you hot in the sunshine?"

"No, Mom," Sydney answered. She didn't think it was necessary to tell her mom about her little brush with the explosion of water.

The cell phone in the pocket of her pink shorts buzzed. Sydney took it out and found a text message from one of her best friends, Elizabeth Anderson. It said: ALMOST PACKED.

Sydney tapped a reply on her keypad: CAN'T W8 TIL U GET HERE.

Sydney and Elizabeth had met at Discovery Lake Camp, and although Elizabeth lived in Texas, they talked every day. Four other girls had been with Sydney and Elizabeth in Cabin 12B. They were Bailey Chang, Alexis Howell, McKenzie Phillips, and Kate Oliver. When camp ended, Kate set up a Web site so the girls could stay in touch. It was password protected, so it was like their own secret cabin in cyberspace. They'd all bought Web cams with babysitting money, chore payments, and allowances so they could see each other and talk online. The Camp Club Girls—as they liked to be called—made Web cam calls, sent IMs, and frequently met in their own private chat rooms.

Sydney continued typing her message: WILL PIC U UP @ D APORT @ 4 2MORO.

"Sydney, I really wish you'd come inside." Sydney's mother crossed her arms.

"Okay, in a few minutes, Mother!" Sydney said without looking up.

The screen door slammed shut.

This was the worst heat wave Washington, D.C., had seen in twenty-five years. Everyone had air conditioners blasting. The energy load was way too much, and the night before, the power had gone out. Sydney hated being in total darkness. She was relieved that today seemed normal.

PACK SHORTS, she typed. REALLY HOT HERE!

While she sat texting, Sydney heard the *thump, thump, thump* of music getting closer and closer. A green jeep raced around the corner, and the booming bass from its stereo echoed inside Sydney's chest. In the passenger seat, Aunt Dee held on to her tan park ranger hat to keep it from flying off of her head. The jeep screeched to a halt in front of Sydney's house, and her aunt hopped out.

"Thanks for the ride, Ben!" she yelled over the music. "See you tomorrow."

The young driver waved and drove off.

GOTTA GO, BETH, Sydney wrote. ANT D'S HOME.

Sydney stood and wiped her feet on the grass. "You're late again," she said. "Mom's mad."

"I know," Aunt Dee apologized. "There was trouble at the Wall." She took off her ranger hat and perched it on Sydney's head. Aunt Dee always blamed her lateness on her job at the Vietnam Veterans Memorial. Sydney didn't understand how she could be so enthusiastic about a long black wall with a bunch of names carved onto it.

"So what was the trouble?" Sydney asked.

"I'll tell you at dinner," said Aunt Dee. She linked her arm through Sydney's. "It's hot out here, girlfriend. Let's go inside."

By the time Sydney washed and sat at her place at the table, Mom and Aunt Dee were already eating. Sydney had learned at camp to pray before every meal. So she bowed her head and said out loud, "Dear Lord, make us truly grateful for this meal and for all the blessings of this day." She noticed that her mom and Aunt Dee stopped eating and bowed their heads, too. "And please keep Dad safe," she said. Sydney always added a blessing for her dad, who was serving in the military overseas.

"Amen!" Mom and Aunt Dee chimed.

Sydney poured iced tea into her tall glass and scooped pasta salad onto her plate. "So what happened at the Wall?" she asked, reaching for a piece of French bread.

"Someone spray-painted the sidewalk last night," Aunt Dee replied. "Graffiti."

Sydney's mom got that look on her face—the one where her forehead turned into wrinkled plastic wrap. "You mean *vandalism*," she said. "I think it's just terrible what kids do these days—"

"How do you know it was kids?" Sydney interrupted. Her mouth was full of creamy macaroni. "Kids aren't the only ones who do bad stuff."

"Don't talk with your mouth full," said Aunt Dee.

"Most times it is," her mom argued. "Just look around our neighborhood." She waved her hand toward the kitchen window. "Vandalism everywhere! Who do you think did all that? Not the adults. The kids don't care about our community. Do they care that this neighborhood used to be a military camp to help slaves that escaped from the South? No! They just want to mess up the nice things that good folks worked so hard to build." Sydney's mother sighed and took a long drink of her iced tea.

Mrs. Lincoln worked at the local historical society, and she was very protective of the neighborhood and its landmarks. She liked to talk about how, in the old days, kids had manners and didn't do anything wrong. Sydney hated it that her mom blamed everything on the kids in the neighborhood.

"There are good kids, too," Sydney argued. "You don't see my friends and me running around spray-painting everything. Give us some credit!" She looked at her plate and pushed the rest of her pasta salad into a neat little pile. "We care what happens."

"We don't know who did it," said Aunt Dee, trying to stop the argument. "Someone painted 'GO 64' in front of panel 30W—in orange paint. Ben and some other volunteers scrubbed it this morning. They'll work on it again tonight when the air cools off some. They're having a hard time cleaning it. Pass the bread, please."

"What does 'GO 64' mean?" Sydney asked, handing her the basket of bread.

11

"That's what we're trying to figure out," Aunt Dee answered. "We're wondering if the number 64 is a clue to who did it. Ben said that in some rap music, 64 means a 1964 Chevrolet Impala. Another volunteer plays chess and said 64 is the number of squares on a chessboard. We don't know what it means."

"Maybe it's Interstate 64," Sydney's mom suggested. "There's construction on that freeway and plenty of orange construction cones. Maybe the orange paint is to protest all that."

"But if it's about the freeway, or a car, or a chessboard, why would they complain by painting graffiti at the Vietnam Wall? Besides, Interstate 64 is in Virginia," Aunt Dee said.

"Yes, but there's some military bases out that way," Mother said. Then she added, "It's probably just kids."

The air-conditioning kicked in again, and a cool draft shot from the air vent, making the kitchen curtains flutter.

"The Wall's lighted at night," Sydney said. "And the park police keep an eye on all the monuments. So why didn't anyone see who did it?"

"The lights were out," Aunt Dee reminded her. "The whole city went dark for a while, and the park police were busy with that. That's when it happened, I'm sure.

Anyway, it's a mess, and we have to clean it up fast. The TV stations are already making a big deal out of it." She dipped her knife into the butter container and slathered butter onto her French bread. "I had such an awful day at work. Everybody blamed everyone else for letting it happen. Like we would *let* it happen! People don't know how hard the Park Service works—"

"May I be excused?" Sydney asked, swallowing her last bite of pasta.

"You may," her mother answered.

Sydney put her dishes into the dishwasher. Then she went upstairs to her room.

The computer on Sydney's desk was on, and her screensaver cast an eerie blue glow on her yellow bedroom walls. Syd's bedroom had no windows, so it was always dark. That was the trouble with living in a row house. If your room was in the middle of the house, you had no windows. She flipped the switch on her desk light and tapped the spacebar on the computer. The monitor lit up, and Sydney noticed that McKenzie Phillips was online. She sent her an IM: *Talk to me?*

The phone icon on the computer screen jiggled back and forth. Sydney clicked on it, and McKenzie's freckled face appeared. She was sitting at the work island in her family's kitchen. "What's up?" she asked.

Sydney turned on her Web cam. "Not much," she said. "I just finished dinner."

"Me, too," McKenzie replied. "Well, almost." She held a slice of cheese pizza in front of her face so Sydney could see it. "We ate early because Dad and Evan have to drive some cattle to pasture. Then they want to practice for the rodeo this weekend." She pointed to the blue baseball cap on her head. Its yellow letters said SULFUR SPRINGS RODEO.

"I didn't want to hang out downstairs," Sydney told her. "Someone spray-painted graffiti by the Vietnam Wall last night, and Mom blamed it on kids again."

McKenzie took a bite out of her pizza. "I saw it on the news. Why did she blame it on kids? I mean, anyone could have done it."

"She blames *everything* on kids," Sydney answered. "I think it's because a lot of the kids around here get into trouble. I try to tell her that we're not all like that, but she doesn't listen. Lately she doesn't listen to anything I say."

"My mom's like that, too," McKenzie said. "Nothing I do is ever right." Her face lit up. "Hey, the news said it was *orange* paint, right?"

"Yeah," Sydney said, fidgeting with her cornrows. "Orange graffiti that said 'GO 64.' So what?"

"So maybe it's some crazy nutcase with Agent Orange."

"Agent who?" Sydney asked.

"Agent Orange!" said McKenzie. "Agent Orange was a chemical they used in Vietnam. I read about it in school. It made some Vietnam soldiers really sick, and some even died. So maybe it wasn't a kid who wrote it. Maybe it's a guy who got Agent Orange, who's mad at the government and wants to get even. By the way, I can't see you well."

"You think too much," Sydney answered. She pulled her desk light closer to her computer and bent it toward her face. "They're trying to figure out what 'GO 64' means. My aunt and mom think it could be about some sort of car, or highway, or maybe even a chessboard—"

"A chessboard!" McKenzie screeched. "A person who plays chess won't spray-paint a national monument."

"I know," Sydney said. "Some gang member probably wrote it. Anyhow, I don't care. I don't want to talk about it anymore."

"I can see you fine now," McKenzie said, changing the subject. "So when is Elizabeth coming?"

"She and her uncle Dan are flying in from Texas tomorrow," Sydney answered. "Aunt Dee and I are going to pick them up at the airport at four. We'll take her uncle to his hotel, and then Elizabeth will come here to stay with us."

"Can Elizabeth's uncle Dan get around all by himself?" McKenzie asked. She twisted a strand of her shoulder-length hair around her fingers. "I mean, he's in a wheelchair and everything."

"As far as I know, he can," Sydney answered. "Elizabeth said he plays wheelchair basketball and competes in wheelchair races, so I suppose he gets around just fine by himself. I'm sure once he gets to the hotel, his Vietnam buddies will help him out if he needs help."

McKenzie reached for a gallon milk container on the kitchen counter. She poured herself a glass. "Well, at least you and Elizabeth don't have to hang around with him the whole time. He'll be busy with his reunion stuff, right?"

"Right," Sydney agreed. "We'll see him Monday at the Vietnam Wall. Aunt Dee wants to give him the tour, and she thinks that Elizabeth and I should be there. Otherwise, we're on our own." Sydney heard strange sounds coming from her computer speakers. "Is that mooing?" she asked.

"Can you hear it?" said McKenzie. "That's Olivia, our old milk cow. About this time every day, she wanders up to the kitchen window and talks to us. I'll move the camera, and you can see her."

McKenzie's face disappeared from the screen. Sydney watched her friend's bare feet move across the kitchen floor as she carried the Web cam to the window. Then a big, black-and-white cow head appeared. Olivia stood chewing her cud and looking at Sydney with huge brown eyes.

"Earth to Mac! Earth to Mac!" Sydney called into her computer's microphone. "Come back, Mac!"

Sydney watched McKenzie's bare feet walk back to the computer. Then her face showed up on the screen.

"Isn't Olivia awesome?" she said. "You really should come to Montana, Syd. We have tons of animals. I know you'd love it, and we could ride horses and hike, just like we did at camp."

"Maybe I will someday," Sydney replied. "But right now, I'm signing off. I want to clean up my room before Elizabeth gets here from Texas. All of my junk is piled on the other bed. If I don't move it, she won't have a place to sleep."

"Okay then," McKenzie said. "I'll sign off, too—and eat more pizza." She picked up the gooey slice from her plate and took another bite. "I'll talk to you tomorrow."

"See ya," Sydney answered, switching off her Web cam.

Everything in her room looked neat except for the other twin bed. It was hardly ever used, so that was where Sydney stored most of her stuff. It held boxes filled with colorful papers and art materials, magazines, piles of clothes, and posters she planned to put up in her room.

Sydney had so much stuff stored there that she didn't know what to do with it all. *Under my bed, I guess,* she thought.

Before long, the bed was cleaned. Sydney changed the sheets. Then she went to her closet and pulled out a new black and tan bedspread that matched her own. She threw it on top of the bed and tucked it neatly around the pillow.

"Sydney?" Aunt Dee stood in the doorway. She held a long white envelope. "This came for you."

The letter was from Elizabeth. Sydney tore open the flap and found a note taped to an information sheet.

Uncle Dan wanted me to send you this so your mom can keep track of him. Just in case of an emergency. It's his reunion schedule.

Sydney Lincoln read the heading on the sheet of paper. It said, "Annual Reunion—64th Transportation Company, Vietnam."

The Wall

Thunderstorms in Texas delayed Elizabeth's flight. By the time Aunt Dee, Sydney, and Elizabeth dropped Uncle Dan off at his hotel and got back to Sydney's house, it was almost midnight.

After the girls got ready for bed, Elizabeth handed Sydney a small package wrapped in polka-dot-covered paper. "I got this for you," she said.

Sydney grinned. She loved getting presents. Carefully she peeled the tape off the paper. Then she reached in and pulled out a square gray box. On the top of it, gold script letters spelled out HIS WORLD, AMARILLO, TEXAS. Sydney opened the lid and found a thick, coppery bangle bracelet. Etched all around it was a scripture verse: *Be strong and courageous. Do not be terrified; do not be discouraged, for the LORD your God will be with you wherever you go. Joshua 1:9.* "This is so cool!" Sydney exclaimed. "Thank you, Beth." She slipped the bracelet over her left wrist.

"My uncle gave me a pendant with that scripture," Elizabeth said. She reached for the pendant on a long silver chain around her neck. Then she held it up so Sydney could see. "It has a special meaning."

Sydney settled into her bed and covered herself with the cool white sheet. "What's the meaning?"

"Well, when Uncle Dan was in Vietnam, he always carried a small Bible in his hip pocket. When he got shot, the bullet went through his pocket and right through the Bible. The doctors said that the Bible slowed down the bullet. If it hadn't, he might have died instead of being paralyzed." Elizabeth stretched out on her own bed and got under the covers. She switched off the light next to her bed. "And do you know what else? In the hospital, Uncle Dan opened his little Bible with the bullet hole, and it fell open to the words, 'Be strong and courageous. Do not be terrified; do not be discouraged, for the Lord your God will be with you wherever you go.' It was Joshua 1:9!"

"Wow," said Sydney. "What a coincidence, huh? Good thing he had the Bible in that pocket."

"Coincidences don't exist," Elizabeth answered. "That was God."

Sydney shut off the light on her nightstand. "Your uncle is lucky to be alive. Maybe he can't walk, but he sure does seem to get around fine. He just zipped around the baggage carousel and grabbed that suitcase. It was—"

"Not that great." Elizabeth finished Sydney's sentence. "Because he still can't walk. I pray every night for God to make him well again. But so far, nothing has happened. If it weren't for you, I wouldn't even have come here with him. Aren't there a lot of statues of soldiers and reminders of wars here? I don't like statues like that. They make me think of Uncle Dan."

Sydney heard tears in her friend's voice. "Washington's not so bad," she said. "We'll go to the Wall first thing tomorrow when Aunt Dee shows your uncle around. Then, the rest of the time, we can do fun stuff."

Elizabeth said nothing.

"Good night, Elizabeth," Sydney said. "Thanks for the bracelet."

"Good night, Sydney," Elizabeth whispered.

•—•—•

The girls got up early the next morning and were glad to find the weather had cooled and left a beautiful, sunny day. They ate breakfast, and then they walked from Sydney's house to the Metro station. From there, they took the Metro, the name everyone called the subway system, to L'Enfant Plaza. They transferred to another train and ended up in a neighborhood west of downtown called Foggy Bottom.

Elizabeth was impressed by how easily Sydney got around. "I'm glad I'm not doing this alone," she said. "You know how directionally disabled I am!"

"Do I!" Sydney replied. "Remember at camp when we were in the woods, and we scared off that cougar? You didn't have a clue where we were. And *you* were the one who'd been to Discovery Lake Camp before!"

They ran up the stairs from the train platform to the street.

"And who got us out of that one?" Sydney added.

"You did!" Elizabeth laughed. "Like I said, I'm directionally disabled."

Quickly they walked a few blocks to the Vietnam Wall.

Elizabeth was surprised to see that the Wall was in a big, grassy park with lots of trees. The girls had agreed to meet Sydney's aunt at the Three Servicemen statue near the west entrance. By the time they got there, Aunt Dee was already telling Uncle Dan and two of his buddies about the memorial.

"The total length of the Wall is 493 feet and 6 inches," Aunt Dee said in her park ranger voice. "Its two arms meet at the central point to make a wide angle of 125 degrees, creating a V shape. One end points toward the Washington Monument and the other end toward the

Lincoln Memorial. The wall is ten feet three inches high at the center and is made of black granite—Oh, hello, girls!"

Uncle Dan and his friends turned to look at Sydney and Elizabeth standing behind them. "Hi, Elizabeth," Uncle Dan said. "Boys, this is my niece, Elizabeth Anderson, and her friend Sydney Lincoln."

The men shook hands with Sydney and Elizabeth. "Are you any relation to Abraham Lincoln?" one of them asked jokingly.

"Not that I know of," said Sydney.

They moved toward the wall as Aunt Dee continued her tour. "The Wall was designed by a young American sculpture artist named Maya Lin."

"Violin," Sydney whispered into Elizabeth's ear. The girls giggled, and Aunt Dee frowned.

"The names of 58,220 men and women are etched into these panels," she said. "You already know these were the men and women killed in the Vietnam War, or listed as missing in action. If you'd like to find specific names, I can help you with that, and our volunteers have tracing paper if you'd like to make tracings of any names. Also, feel free to leave a note or other memento at the Wall. People leave things here every day, like these—" She hesitated. "Oranges?"

A row of oranges lined the base of the Wall. Actually, they were tangerines, but Sydney kept that fact to herself. Aunt Dee got annoyed when Sydney corrected her about such facts. The tangerines were neatly placed about three feet apart, stopping halfway down the west part of the Wall.

"We've had some strange things left here lately," Aunt Dee said. "Last week, it was lemons."

"Lemons?" Uncle Dan chuckled. "That does seem strange."

"I know," Aunt Dee answered. "They were arranged in a neat little pyramid in front of panel 4E. The week before that, a box of blueberries was left by 48W; and the week before that, a row of limes led to panel 14W. They were set there just like these oranges."

"Tangerines!" Sydney corrected her. She couldn't help herself.

"Whatever," Aunt Dee replied. "And then, of course, the other day some vandals struck."

"I heard about that on the news," said one of the buddies. "It made me mad that someone disrespected the Wall like that. Did they catch them yet?"

"No," Aunt Dee answered. "Since it was graffiti, we think it was kids, probably some gang members. Most cities seem to have that problem."

Sydney and Elizabeth walked away, leaving the adults to discuss gang activities and whatever else people their age talked about.

"This place is so quiet and depressing," Elizabeth observed.

Sydney agreed. "A lot of people treat it like it's a cemetery. I don't come here unless Aunt Dee needs me to. . . . Too many sad people. But we have to hang around until your uncle and his friends leave."

"I guess," said Elizabeth.

"Then we can walk to the Tidal Basin and ride the paddle boats," Sydney continued. "That'll be fun."

The girls wandered along the Wall with groups of tourists. They noticed all the different things left by people who wanted to remember the dead soldiers: a teddy bear here, a pair of combat boots there, letters addressed to loved ones, identification tags soldiers had worn in Vietnam, and plenty of tiny American flags. Nearby, a man was busy making a rubbing of one of the names on the Wall. Not far from him, an old woman laid a red rose on the brick walkway in front of one of the panels.

When they were about halfway down the west side of the Wall, Elizabeth noticed her uncle and his friends behind them. Uncle Dan had his head in his hands. He seemed to be crying, and each buddy had an arm around him. Elizabeth looked away. She couldn't stand to see her uncle being sad. Bitter anger crept up inside of her. *"Refrain from anger and turn from wrath; do not fret— it leads only to evil,"* she reminded herself. *Psalm 37:8.* The shiny granite wall reflected images like a mirror, so Elizabeth stopped to put a clip in her long blond hair.

Sydney was next to her by panel 30W, setting up a little American flag that had toppled over. She saw a tall man approaching them. He looked about the same age as Tyler, Sydney's brother, who was away at college. The man's fair cheeks and chin were almost hidden by his bushy red beard, and Sydney noticed that he smelled like cigarette smoke. His blue T-shirt was stained and his black cargo shorts were too big for him. He wore shabby brown sandals at the ends of his long, sunburned legs. Each was decorated with a silver peace sign about the size of a quarter.

The man read the names on the wall. Then he picked up the last tangerine in the long row of them. He tossed it into the air and caught it in his right hand. "This is the place, Moose," he said.

A big, burly guy had sauntered next to him. His head was shaved and his walnut-colored eyes darted about as he scanned the names on panel 30W. His gray T-shirt showed the picture of a fierce bulldog with the words NICE DOGGY.

"You're right, Rusty," he said. "Looks like they got the sidewalk cleaned up already. Good thing there was a picture in the paper." He took a handkerchief out of his pocket and blew his nose.

"Yeah, these guys work fast," Rusty muttered. "Bet it took a lot of scrubbing." He reached down and picked up a note someone had attached to a flag by the wall. He read it aloud. "Patience is bitter, but it bears sweet fruit." He laughed. "The Professor has a sense of humor. I think I'll eat my orange now."

Sydney wanted to say that they were tangerines, not oranges. Instead, she and Elizabeth listened while trying not to be obvious.

Moose retied the laces on his dirty tennis shoes. "This one was a little different from green, blue, and yellow," he said. "But I didn't have to look long before I found it, Rusty. You saw it, too, right?"

Rusty peeled the tangerine and stuffed the peelings into his pocket. Then he gave the fruit to his friend. "Yeah, I saw it, Moose. Right away."

"Saw what?" Elizabeth whispered to Sydney.

Sydney shrugged.

Moose bit into the tangerine. Juice ran down his chin, trickled onto his hairy arms, and dripped onto his shirt. When he finished eating, he wiped his sticky hands on his jeans. "We should probably leave something for The Professor, so he knows when—"

"Shut up," Rusty grunted.

"But we have to—"

"Shut. . .up!" Rusty whispered, spitting out each word. He tipped his head slightly toward Sydney and Beth. Then he nodded toward the other tourists.

"I get it," Moose said. He sounded like he'd just discovered the answer to a riddle. He faced the Wall. Then, after about thirty seconds and a quick jab in the ribs from Rusty, he saluted. "We should leave something nice for our dearly departed fellow soldier," he said loudly.

Rusty picked up another tangerine and tossed it to Moose. "Let's go sit down and have a snack," he directed.

The two men walked away.

"What do you think that was about?" Elizabeth asked.

"Beats me," Sydney answered. "But we should walk; otherwise they might think it's weird that we're standing here for so long."

The girls strolled toward the center of the Wall, the place where the West Wall met the East. Uncle Dan and his buddies were halfway down the East Wall, and one of the buddies was kneeling on the ground making a tissue paper rubbing of a name.

"I think those guys were creepy," Elizabeth said. "They were obviously looking for something and found it. Who do you think The Professor is?" Elizabeth was so busy thinking and talking that she almost bumped into a lady in front of her.

"And that stuff about this one being different from green, blue, and yellow," Sydney added. "You're right. They were kind of creepy."

"Maybe we should tell your aunt," said Elizabeth. "I think they're up to something. Maybe they're the guys who painted the graffiti on the sidewalk."

Sydney stopped in front of panel 10E and pretended to search for a name. "No, I don't think so, Beth. I hate to admit it, but kids probably did the graffiti. And I don't think we should tell my aunt. I mean, they weren't doing anything wrong."

"But they were acting suspicious," Elizabeth argued as she joined Sydney and pretended to look for a name on the shiny black panel.

"Think about it. *We* might look suspicious," Sydney suggested. "We've been standing here for five minutes acting like we're looking for a name. Not exactly what a couple of kids would do."

The girls walked to Elizabeth's uncle and his friends.

"There you are!" Uncle Dan said. "Listen, we're almost done. Would you girls like to have lunch with the boys and me?"

Sydney looked at Elizabeth.

"I'm buying," Uncle Dan said, smiling.

"Well, okay," Elizabeth replied. "How about if we meet you by the statue of the ladies when you're done?"

"You mean the statue of the *nurses*," one of the buddies corrected her. "We can tell you some stories about them over lunch." He grinned and winked at Uncle Dan.

"Okay, we'll meet you over there," Sydney said. "Let's go, Elizabeth!" She linked her arm with her friend's and tugged on it, pulling Elizabeth back toward the center of the Wall.

"What?" Elizabeth balked.

"Look." Sydney pointed toward the middle of the West Wall. Moose and Rusty were back, putting something near the bottom of panel 30W.

"Slow down," Elizabeth said. "Let them leave it, and then we'll see what it is."

The girls stopped walking and pretended again to look for a name on the Wall.

"Okay, they're leaving," Elizabeth reported. "Let's *slowly* walk down there so we don't draw attention to ourselves."

The girls strolled toward panel 30W. When they got there, they found a note written on lined notebook paper. It was stuck onto the thin plastic stick of a small American flag. Elizabeth knelt down and read it aloud. "Meade me in St. Louis, July 1."

"Huh?" Sydney bent down to see.

"That's what it says," Elizabeth told her. "All in capital letters. 'MEADE ME IN ST. LOUIS, JULY 1.'" She hesitated for a few seconds. "Sydney? Do you know how it is when God puts a thought in your head and you know that it's true? Well, I just got one of those thoughts, and it's not good!"

Elizabeth felt a heavy hand rest on her shoulder.

"It's time to go, little girl," a man's voice ordered.

The Lincoln Memorial

Elizabeth's heart jumped to her throat. She whirled around. Uncle Dan stood behind her.

"Did I scare you, honey?" he said. "I'm sorry. Are you ready to go to lunch?"

Elizabeth brushed some dirt from the knees of her new blue jeans. "You know what, Uncle Dan? I think Sydney and I will skip lunch today. I really want to see stuff in Washington, D.C., and we're only here for a week."

What? Sydney thought. She was looking forward to a free lunch in the city. Most of the time when her family went out to eat, it was to a place in her neighborhood called Ben's Chili Bowl. Anywhere else was a treat.

Uncle Dan looked disappointed but didn't try to persuade the girls any further.

The girls walked with Uncle Dan and his friends to the west end of the Vietnam Wall to say their good-byes.

"Check in with me this week," Uncle Dan told his

niece. "Your mom will be furious if I don't take good care of you."

One of his buddies, Al, chuckled. "And we'll take good care of your uncle," he said. Al was the one who had corrected Elizabeth about the nurses' statue. Elizabeth didn't like something about him.

She kissed her uncle on the forehead. "Don't worry, Uncle Dan. I'll be fine."

The men had barely walked away when Sydney said, "You know, a free lunch sounded pretty good to me."

Elizabeth took Sydney's arm and pulled her. "We have to find Rusty and Moose," she said. "I think they went that way." She pointed toward the Lincoln Memorial.

The girls started walking along Henry Bacon Drive toward the big white building with the famous statue of Abraham Lincoln.

"When I read the words 'Meade me in St. Louis,' well, I got a thought," Elizabeth said. "If I'm right, those guys are terrorists."

"What!" Sydney shrieked. "They're weird and creepy, but they don't look like terrorists."

A police car rushed past them, weaving through traffic on the drive. Its siren briefly interrupted their conversation.

"Remember that Bible verse: 'Outside you look good,

but inside you are evil and only pretend to be good'?" Elizabeth asked.

"No," Sydney answered. "Why do you know so much scripture?"

"Because just about everybody in my family is a minister or a missionary," Elizabeth said.

The girls split up and walked around two ladies pushing baby strollers.

Elizabeth had to run a few steps to catch up with Sydney. "As soon as I read those words, 'Meade me in St. Louis,' I thought about a few years ago when terrorists tried to assassinate President Meade. Do you remember? It was at the Smithsonian, at the National Air and Space Museum. Slow down a little, please."

Sydney never did anything slowly. Her friends often had a hard time keeping up with her fast, long legs. "Oh yeah," she answered. "The president was there to celebrate some sort of anniversary."

"The anniversary of Charles Lindberg's flight across the Atlantic in his plane, The Spirit of St. Louis," Elizabeth added.

"I almost forgot about that," Sydney continued. She walked a little slower. "That was the first year that Meade was president. Someone tried to shoot him but got away, and the government said it was terrorists. The Spirit of

St. Louis. . .President Meade. . . Elizabeth! You don't think the note was about that?"

"They never caught who did it," Elizabeth reminded her. "I think Rusty and Moose might at least know something about that."

The girls passed a crowd of people at a food cart near the Lincoln Memorial. Sydney suddenly realized how hungry she was.

"You and the rest of the Camp Club Girls always accuse me of jumping to conclusions," she said. "But this time, I think *you're* jumping to conclusions. Even if you *are* right, Moose and Rusty are gone by now. We'll never find them in this crowd. And since you cost me a free lunch today, let's get in line and buy some sandwiches."

"Okay," Elizabeth replied. "But I wish I knew where they went."

When the girls finally got their food and drinks, they sat on a bench facing the street. The Lincoln Memorial towered to their left, almost one hundred feet tall. Its huge white columns made it look like an ancient Greek temple.

Sydney peeled the paper off her BLT wrap and took a bite. "As long as we're here, do you want to tour the memorial?" she asked.

"Not really," Elizabeth said as she opened her chocolate

milk. "Did you know that a long time ago, Vietnam War protests went on at the Lincoln Memorial? Being here reminds me of what happened to my uncle Dan."

"Elizabeth," Sydney groaned. "You can't visit Washington, D.C., and not see the monuments. Sure, there have been protests here, but that's not what it's all about."

Elizabeth said nothing. It was just like the night before when they'd been talking about Uncle Dan before going to bed.

"This place is a memorial to the president who freed the slaves. Martin Luther King Jr. made his famous 'I Have a Dream' speech here, and Marian Anderson sang here when they wouldn't let her sing in Constitution Hall because she was black. I like the Lincoln Memorial, Elizabeth. Some really good things happened here!"

Sydney didn't like being annoyed with her friend, but she couldn't understand Elizabeth's attitude. She was always easygoing and understanding, but since she'd arrived, she just didn't seem to be herself.

"I'm sorry," Elizabeth apologized. She picked at her burrito with a black plastic fork. "I just don't understand why people have to fight in wars where good folks get hurt—like my uncle."

Sydney thought hard for something to say. "Wars have happened since way back in Old Testament times, Beth.

Remember when David fought Goliath? Can you try not to think about bad stuff and just have a good time?" She offered her friend a dill pickle.

Elizabeth screwed up her face. "No, thank you," she said.

A shiny black limousine pulled up in front of them. It stopped on the wrong side of the street and held up traffic. The driver got out and walked briskly toward the back door.

"Wow," said Elizabeth. "Who do you think is in there?"

Sydney took the last bite of her wrap and tossed the container into a trash can by the bench. "Probably a senator or a congressman. You see tons of limos in the District."

The driver opened the back door, and a short, dark man in a black suit got out. His crisp white shirt gleamed against his tan skin, and a thin black necktie hung neatly inside the front of his suit jacket. His mirrored sunglasses reflected the image of Sydney and Elizabeth sitting on the bench nearby. "Twenty minutes," he said to the driver. He walked toward the memorial, and the limo drove off.

Sydney turned around to look at him. "Elizabeth!" she gasped.

"What?"

"There are Rusty and Moose."

Sure enough, Moose and Rusty stood on the sidewalk, not far from where Sydney and Elizabeth sat. The girls watched the man in the suit approach them. Moose stuck out his hand for the man to shake it, but the man ignored him. Then all three walked briskly toward the Lincoln Memorial.

"Let's see what they're up to," Sydney said.

"But you think they're good, upstanding citizens," Elizabeth reminded her.

"I didn't say that," Sydney argued. "I said that they don't look like terrorists. It won't hurt to check them out. Maybe you're right. Maybe they did have something to do with the graffiti."

The men were a good distance ahead of them now. The girls wove through the crowd trying to keep them in sight. Sydney, being taller than Elizabeth, focused on Rusty's shaggy red hair. The short man was impossible to see. He was dwarfed by Moose's big, hulking body.

"Do you see them?" Elizabeth asked. She walked a few steps on her tiptoes.

"I see the top of Rusty's head bobbing up and down," Sydney answered. "Looks like they're heading for the stairs."

The Lincoln Memorial had fifty-six wide marble stairs leading to the statue of the sixteenth president

38

of the United States. People sat on the staircase talking and reading. Tourists climbed to the top to gaze at the Reflecting Pool on the Mall and, beyond it, the Washington Monument and the United States Capitol Building.

The men started to climb the stairs.

"Now what?" Elizabeth asked.

"We should try to get close enough to listen and find out, once and for all, if they're up to something," Sydney told her. "But we'll have to be careful that they don't see us. They might remember us."

"How about if we split up?" Elizabeth suggested. "They're less likely to recognize us if we're not together."

The men were halfway up the stairs now.

"Good idea," Sydney agreed. "But let's keep an eye on each other. Just in case."

The girls split up. Elizabeth ran up the left side of the staircase, and Sydney ran up the right.

At the top of the stairs, a sign read QUIET, RESPECT PLEASE. Just beyond it was the nineteen-foot-tall statue of President Lincoln. He towered over the tourists, looking relaxed but alert, sitting in his chair, watching over the nation's capital. Moose, Rusty, and the short man didn't seem to notice the president. They whisked past him as if he wasn't even there.

The memorial was surrounded by thirty-six huge

columns. They were thirty-seven feet tall and fat enough to hide behind. Sydney saw the men hurry to the column farthest to the right of the president. They disappeared around it.

Sydney searched for Elizabeth and saw her standing at the foot of the Lincoln statue. She was watching Sydney like a hawk. Sydney pointed to herself and then toward the column where the men went, showing Elizabeth that she would follow them. Elizabeth put her right index finger to her lips.

Silently, like a shadow, Sydney slipped from one marble column to the next. Finally she was just one column away. It would be tricky to shift to the last column where the men were standing. If the men changed their position, she would be caught. Sydney peeked around the column to be sure the coast was clear. She said a short prayer and took a deep breath. Then she slithered to the column hiding the men. With her back plastered against the pillar just a few feet from where they stood, Sydney listened.

"We left a note for you," Moose was saying, "because we didn't expect you to show up."

The short man snickered. "You never know when I'll show up." His deep voice didn't fit his small, slim body. "That's why you'd better do exactly what you're told."

"We are, boss!" Rusty spoke this time. His voice was almost a whisper, nervous and hushed. "We're doing it just like you told us to."

"That's good," said the man. "Otherwise, we might have to send you on the trip with Meade."

What does that *mean?* Sydney wondered. She pressed tighter against the marble pillar and shifted, ever so slightly, to her left. She tried to listen even harder.

"*Waaaaaaaaaa!*" A high-pitched shriek filled the air. Sydney's heart stopped as she looked toward the Lincoln statue. A woman near Elizabeth was trying to calm her unhappy little boy. As Elizabeth and Sydney watched, the mother led her screaming child down the steps and away from the president's statue. Sydney sighed.

"Who came up with the tattoo idea?" The short man was talking now. Sydney had missed part of the conversation.

"I did, boss," Moose said uncertainly.

There was a short pause.

"Good work," he said. "I didn't think you had it in you, Percival."

Percival! Sydney thought to herself. *Moose's real name is Percival?* She stifled a laugh. What a funny, old-fashioned name!

"Thanks, boss!" Moose's voice relaxed.

"Don't you want us to go check out the place?" asked Rusty. "We could go right now."

"I warned you about being impatient," the short man snapped. "I'll talk it over with him first. If it's a go, then we'll move up to the next level. When that happens, *then* you can go and check it out."

"Tomorrow?" Rusty asked.

"Tomorrow," the man said.

Sydney saw Elizabeth with her right arm in the air. Beth was frantically making counter-clockwise circles with her right hand. Sydney heard footsteps on the opposite side of the pillar. The men were leaving. She inched her way counter-clockwise around the gigantic column, making sure she was opposite of where they were. If they saw her, she couldn't imagine what would happen.

Sydney held her breath and didn't let it out until she was sure they were gone. She peeked around the back of the column and looked toward Elizabeth. The men were almost to her, but she had her back to them. She was talking with a group of old ladies, trying to edge her way in front of them as she pointed up at the Lincoln statue. *She's acting like a tour guide so they won't recognize her,* Sydney thought. The men walked by, not seeing Elizabeth, and continued down the stairs.

Sydney came out from her hiding place and hurried toward her friend.

"And if you'd like to learn more about the Lincoln Memorial, you can ask one of the park rangers down there." Elizabeth pointed down the steps toward the Reflecting Pool where a ranger, wearing a uniform like Aunt Dee's, was talking with tourists. The women started down the stairs.

"So what did they say?" Elizabeth asked.

"I don't have a good feeling about them," Sydney confided. "Moose and Rusty called the suit guy 'Boss,' and they seemed afraid of him. They were extra polite. The suit guy said Meade is taking a trip, and if Moose and Rusty don't do what they're told, they might go with him. They talked about a tattoo and taking things to the next level, and they asked the boss if they should go check someplace out. But I don't know where that is. Something's happening tomorrow, too, but I don't know that either. And would you believe that Moose's real name is Percival?"

"*Percival!* Do you think the suit guy is The Professor?" Elizabeth asked.

"I don't know," Sydney said. "But I think it's too late for us to go to the Smithsonian now. And I think we should tell the other Camp Club Girls what's going on and see what they think. Let's text McKenzie and ask her to schedule a group chat for tonight."

"Great idea," Elizabeth responded. "Especially since all the time I watched you, I felt someone was watching *me!*"

CHAPTER 4

Colors of Danger!

Promptly at 6:55 that night, Sydney was waiting at her computer with Elizabeth seated next to her. She entered the Camp Club Girls' chat room, and right away, the messages began to arrive.

Alexis: *Are you guys ok? I got an uncomfortable feeling about you today and prayed for you.*

Sydney: *When everyone logs on, we'll explain all.*

McKenzie: *I'm here. I bet something to do with Agent Orange is involved.*

Alexis: *Let's hope it's just kids playing a prank and not something worse. However, I did see a mystery movie last week that had terrorists masquerading as kids.*

Kate: *Biscuit started barking like crazy as soon as I pulled up this screen. I think he knows it's you guys, and is trying to tell you he misses you.*

Sydney: *How is Biscuit? I wish he could text with us.*

Kate: *He's wanted to play ball with me all day.*

Bailey: *I'm here! Just got home from a day with Mom in Chicago. Good thing we came home early. We're an hour behind you here in Peoria.*

McKenzie: *I was beginning to wonder if you were home when I sent an e-mail and didn't hear from you.*

Sydney: *Okay, since we're all here, let's get started. . . .*

●—●—●

Sydney spent the next few minutes telling the girls about all that had happened that day. She told them about Moose and Rusty and everything that had gone on at the Wall that morning. Then she explained how she had listened to their conversation at the Lincoln Memorial.

Elizabeth took the keyboard and slid it over to where she sat next to Sydney at her desk.

Elizabeth: *When I read the note,* "Meade me in St. Louis, July 1," *the Lord gave me the memory of President Meade and when he was almost shot a few years back. It was at the National Air and Space Museum at the Smithsonian Museum, here in Washington. The president was there to honor Lindberg's*

*flight in his plane, the Spirit of St. Louis. So
I've been wondering, do you think they could
be planning something evil at the same place
on July 1st?*

Alexis: *Are you sure that the thought was from
God, Elizabeth? Sometimes Satan gives us
thoughts to throw us off track. You probably
know where the Bible says that.*

Elizabeth: *It's in 2 Corinthians: "Even Satan tries
to make himself look like an angel of light. So
why does it seem strange for Satan's servants to
pretend to do what is right?" But, Alex, I know
that this thought was from God. Oh, and I
forgot to tell you about the fruit.*

Bailey: *Fruit? This is beginning to sound really
crazy, Lizzybet.*

Elizabeth: *I know. Someone has been leaving
fruit at the Vietnam Wall: a small pyramid of
lemons, a box of blueberries, and rows of limes
and oranges.*

Sydney took the keyboard back.

Sydney: *Tangerines!*
McKenzie: *I think the fruit is important. That one*

guy found the note about patience being bitter
and bearing sweet fruit."

Kate: *I looked that up online. It's a Turkish
proverb. Whoever wrote it might want those
guys to be patient about whatever they're up to.*

Bailey: *That one guy's name is Red. Why? What
do they look like?*

Elizabeth: *Moose and* Rusty, *that's his name, look
messy, like they haven't combed their hair or
washed their clothes in a while. The short guy. . .
well. . .think of an FBI agent. He looks like that.*

McKenzie: *Rusty said, "This one is different from
green, blue, and yellow." Think about it. Limes
are green, blueberries are blue, lemons are
yellow.*

Sydney: *And* tangerines *are orange! But what do
those colors mean. . .if anything?*

Kate: *Was the fruit always left in the same spot?*

Sydney turned to Elizabeth. "Do you know?"

Elizabeth twisted the pendant on her necklace. "It
wasn't in the same spot," she said. "I remember your
aunt told Uncle Dan where they left it, but I wasn't
really listening. Why don't you ask her? But don't be
too obvious about it."

"Okay," Sydney replied. "I'll get a banana from the kitchen. Then I'll use that to start a conversation. I'll say that it reminded me of the fruit at the Wall. Aunt Dee will love it if I ask her. She likes talking about her work."

Sydney pushed the keyboard back to Elizabeth and hurried downstairs to find Aunt Dee.

The other girls chatted for a while as they waited for Sydney to return. Elizabeth told them a little about her uncle and that he had been wounded in Vietnam. She asked them all to pray that the Lord would heal Uncle Dan's legs so he could walk again.

Suddenly Sydney burst back into the room repeating, "4E, 48W, 14W." She took the keyboard from Elizabeth.

Sydney: *Write this down. 4E lemons, 48W blueberries, 14W limes.*

Kate: *And the oranges were where?*

Elizabeth: *They were in a long row from the beginning of the Wall to the same place where the graffiti was painted on the sidewalk— panel 30W.*

Kate: *Everyone go to* www.viewthewall.com/ demo_wallbrowse.htm. *Let me know when you're there.*

Sydney: *We're there.*

McKenzie: *Me, too.*

Bailey: *And me.*

Alexis: *Hang on. My browser is acting up. I have to try it again. Okay, I'm in. Now what?*

Kate: *Click on any panel number and it will take you to a photograph of that panel on the Wall. Then you can zoom in and read the names on the panel. I think that's what we need to do. We need to read each panel where the fruits were left, and look for clues.*

McKenzie: *That will take forever! I think we should research Agent Orange. That's the obvious answer.*

Alexis: *Maybe the obvious answer isn't the one we need. I think we should check out Kate's idea. Then, if that doesn't work, we can check out Agent Orange.*

Sydney clicked on panel 4E. A photo popped up of that panel on the Vietnam Wall. She and Elizabeth began reading the hundreds of names on the panel.

Sydney: *There are 136 rows. Why don't we divide them up? It'll go faster that way.*

She assigned each girl a group of rows.

> Bailey: *What am I supposed to be looking for?*
> Sydney: *Any name that might connect with lemons. Think about what they look like, how they taste, that sort of stuff.*

"I don't like doing this," Elizabeth told Sydney. "All of these names represent someone who was killed in Vietnam. This is more than just a list of names; it's real people."

"I know," Sydney agreed as she searched the rows. "I don't like doing it either."

> Bailey: *I think I might have found something. I see someone with the last name* Gold *in row 34. Lemons are sort of gold.*
> Alexis: *That's great work, Bailey! I wrote that down. Lemons, gold, row 34, panel 4E.*
> Kate: *Did anyone else find anything? If not, let's move to the next panel, 48W. Look for anything that connects to blue or blueberries.*

Again Sydney assigned rows, and she and Elizabeth searched their lists of names. Before long, McKenzie's name popped on the screen.

> McKenzie: *I think Bailey might be on to something.
> A soldier is on my list with the last name* Blue*!*
> Kate: *I'm looking on panel 14W, where the limes
> were. There's a Green on my list.*

Sydney shrugged her shoulders and looked at Elizabeth. "If there's a soldier named Tangerine on panel 30W, I'll make your bed the rest of the time you're here," she promised. Sydney figured that it was a safe promise to make, because no one, especially not a soldier, would be named Tangerine.

> Bailey: *I'm on 30W. And guess what? I found a
> guy named Orange.*
> Sydney: *Oh, come on, Bailey. No one is named
> Orange. I mean, have you ever met any
> Oranges?*
> Alexis: *Bailey is right. And this one is different
> from Green, Blue, and Yellow. . .I mean Gold.
> Orange is his* first *name.*

Sydney clicked to the photograph of panel 30W. Sure enough, there was a man named Orange.

McKenzie: *And do you see* where *it is? Row 64. That's what 64 means in* "GO 64." *It was a clue for Rusty and Moose to look at that row. The leader must have thought that they needed some extra help, since this name is a little different from the others.*

Elizabeth took the keyboard from Sydney.

Elizabeth: *So we know the boss, or professor, or whoever he is, was telling Rusty and Moose to look for colors. But why?*

Kate: *You'll never believe this. I was doing a search for colors, and Biscuit put his red ball in my lap.*

Bailey: *Pet Biscuit for me!*

Sydney: *What's hard to believe about Biscuit putting his ball in your lap?*

Kate: *The ball is red. I pushed it out of my lap as I was typing a search for the colors we talked about. When I saw the red ball bouncing, I accidentally typed in red, too. Guess what! These colors are the colors of the Homeland Security Terror Alert System. Green is a low risk of terrorist attacks. Blue is a general risk*

Camp Club Girls

of attacks. Yellow means a significant risk of attacks. And orange is a high risk. There's only one more level above that, and it's red—a severe risk of terrorist attacks!

Elizabeth looked at Sydney, and Sydney knew what she was thinking.

Elizabeth: *That's what the short man meant when he told Moose and Rusty that they'd be taking things to the next level.*

Sydney grabbed the keyboard back.

Sydney: *Oh my goodness! They really are terrorists!*

54

A Plan to Track Trouble

The next morning, Sydney and Elizabeth were at Union Station in Washington, D.C., waiting for Kate Oliver to arrive. She was on the ten o'clock train from Philadelphia. During their group chat the night before, Kate had come up with a brilliant idea that involved a piece of electronic equipment. Since Philadelphia was only a few hours away and trains ran frequently up and down the coast, the girls had decided she would join Sydney and Elizabeth. If all went well, they would put her idea into action before the terrorists stepped up their plan to Level Red.

The old, cavernous train building was alive with activity. Its white marble floors echoed with the footsteps of tourists, people on business, and government workers as they rushed to and from their trains. Music drifted from stores on the upper level, adding to the chaos.

Sydney stood by the doors nearest the train tracks to the Philadelphia–Washington, D.C., line. Kate's train would arrive at that platform.

Sydney and Elizabeth opened the big glass doors that led out to the tracks. A blast of air, heavy with the smell of diesel fuel, swept past the girls' faces. They waited and watched while some trains sat idle on the tracks and others chugged in and out of the station.

Sydney soon spotted a single headlight on the Philadelphia track. Slowly an enormous, shiny, bullet-shaped engine chugged into the station pulling six cars behind it. It stopped at the platform where the girls waited. The doors slid open, and passengers spilled out and scurried into the building like ants toward a crumb.

"Do you see Kate?" Sydney asked.

"Not yet," Elizabeth replied.

The crowd was thinning out. Only a dozen or so people remained. The girls worried that Kate had missed her train, but then they saw her. She waved to them as she exited the third car and stepped onto the concrete platform. She ran toward them, her sandy-colored hair bouncing. With her yellow T-shirt, fuchsia backpack, and bright green shorts, she looked as if she'd stepped off a tropical island.

"Hi, Syd. Hi, Elizabeth," Kate said. She briefly hugged each friend.

"We were afraid you missed the train," Sydney said as they walked into the crowded station.

"I was listening to Casting Crowns on my iPod," Kate answered. "I decided to hang out on the train until most people got off. It was a zoo in there."

Sydney led the girls down the escalators to the street level of the station. Then they walked toward the Plaza exit. "We'll go to West Potomac Park," Sydney announced. "Then we can talk."

Kate and Elizabeth scurried, trying to keep up with Sydney's long stride.

"I have the equipment ready," Kate announced. "I just have to show you how to use it. Do you have the rest of the stuff?"

"Yes. In my backpack," Elizabeth answered.

They were outside Union Station now and walking across the Plaza. They passed the Columbus Memorial Fountain where the statue of Christopher Columbus stared steely-eyed into the distance. To the right of him was a carving of a bearded man, sitting. To the left of him was a carving of an American Indian from long ago, crouching behind his shield and reaching for an arrow.

The friends caught a city bus on Constitution Avenue. Cars, taxis, and delivery vans whizzed beside them as they traveled west to 15th Street. They got off on 15th and walked toward the Washington Monument. Then they covered the short distance to the Tidal Basin in the park.

The girls found a quiet bench under the cherry trees. Nearby, children and grown-ups rode paddleboats through the cool, clear water in the Tidal Basin. In the peaceful setting, no one could have known that Kate, Elizabeth, and Sydney were worried about a terrorist attack on President Meade.

Kate unzipped her backpack and pulled out a small black cell phone. "Here it is," she said. "I've programmed it so any of us can access the data from our computers. It works like this: We have to make sure that this phone is with Moose all the time. From what you said, he's the dumber of the two, so it'll be easier to get him to take it. As long as he has this phone, we can track him wherever he goes."

Kate handed Sydney and Elizabeth each a slip of paper with some writing on it. "When you get home, just go to this URL and type in your password. Elizabeth, yours is 'Indiana.' Sydney, yours is 'Jones.' Once you do that, you'll see a screen with a map on it. It will show you exactly where Moose is. He'll appear as a little green blip on the screen."

Sydney laughed when she thought of the big, hulking Moose as nothing more than a small green blip.

Elizabeth opened her yellow backpack and took out the box that Sydney's bracelet had come in. Then she pulled out a brown paper lunch bag, a pair of scissors, and a roll of tape. "I have everything we need," she said.

Kate handed Elizabeth the phone, and carefully Elizabeth placed it into the box. She cut the paper bag and made it into a piece of wrapping paper. Then she folded it around the box and sealed it with tape.

"Now we have to create the note," Sydney began. "I know what we should say."

"You dictate and I'll write," Kate offered, taking a black permanent marker out of her backpack.

"Okay, here goes." Sydney dictated the words and Kate wrote them on a leftover scrap of the paper bag:

Moose, it is very important *that you keep this package with you at all times. DO NOT OPEN IT or talk to anyone about it, including people you trust—not even the person giving you this! You will be asked for this package at the end of your mission. Keep it safe, keep quiet, or else!*

"That sounds good!" Kate said, smiling.

"I think so, too," Elizabeth agreed. "From what Sydney overheard at the Lincoln Memorial, Moose seems to want to please the guy in the suit. So he'll probably take very good care of this package."

She folded the note in half, hiding the message inside. Then she wrote "Moose" on the blank side and taped it to the top of the wrapped box.

"We should go now," she said. "Idle hands are the devil's playground."

"Is that in the Bible?" Sydney asked.

"No, but it's a good proverb," Elizabeth replied.

Within moments, the girls arrived at the Vietnam Wall. When the friends got there, they found the place crowded with visitors.

The girls hid near the trees at the south yard of the Wall.

"Kate, I think you should do this alone," Sydney suggested. "Moose and Rusty have never seen you. So if you run into them, it'll be no big deal. Plus, if my aunt is around and she sees us, she'll wonder why we're here."

"I think you're right," Kate said. She dropped her backpack on the ground. "Watch my stuff."

Elizabeth handed her the small package wrapped in brown paper. Then Kate went toward the Wall.

Sydney and Elizabeth stayed hidden in trees. Sydney had brought a pair of binoculars she liked to use for bird watching. She was peering through them, watching Kate.

Kate purposefully looked indifferent as she casually strolled past the panels etched with names. On the west end, the panels began with the number 70. Only five names were etched onto that first panel. It was the shortest one on the west part of the Wall. Each panel beyond it stood a little bit taller until the east and west walls met in the middle at their highest points. Kate walked on past panels 61. . .60. . .59. . .58. . .57. Then something caught her eye. She hurried to a spot five panels down.

"Hey, she's stopping!" said Sydney, squinting through the binoculars.

"She must be there," Elizabeth added.

"No. She's a long way away from it still," Sydney disagreed.

Sydney watched as Kate stopped in front of a quart-sized box of huge red strawberries on the ground at the center of panel 52W.

"She's at the wrong panel!" Sydney exclaimed. "Didn't we agree that she'd leave the box by panel 30W?"

"Yes," Elizabeth confirmed.

"Well, she's a long way from there," Sydney said, focusing her binoculars.

"What's she doing now?" Elizabeth wondered. She could see Kate crouching down in front of the Wall.

"I don't know. I can't tell, because she has her back to me. I think she might be leaving the package there," said Sydney.

"But it's the wrong place!" Elizabeth said with exasperation.

"Oh, Elizabeth! What are we going to do? Come on, girl!" Sydney said under her breath. "You're at the wrong spot!"

The girls watched as Kate set the package down.

"I'm going in," Sydney exclaimed, handing the binoculars to Elizabeth.

"Do you think that's a good idea?" Elizabeth asked nervously.

"Probably not, but I'll be careful. If that phone gets into the wrong hands, we're sunk. Keep an eye on us." Sydney sprinted across the grass toward the Wall.

Just as Kate stood up, she felt someone grab her arm. She jumped.

"What are you doing?" Sydney whispered. "This is the wrong place."

"No, it's not!" Kate whispered back. "Let's not talk about it here."

"But this isn't 30W!" Sydney reminded her. "It's down that way." She pointed to her left.

"Don't point!" Kate scolded. "Someone might be watching us. Let's get out of here."

Sydney was about to cut across the grass again.

"Uh-uh," Kate said. She took Sydney by the arm.

"You'll show them where we're hiding!" Kate was right. Obediently, Sydney followed her to the entrance to the memorial. They doubled back toward the trees where Elizabeth was.

"I knew what I was doing!" Kate said when they were away from the crowd. "As I walked to panel 30W, I saw a box of strawberries by panel 52W. I had to check it out."

The girls were approaching Elizabeth now. She was still watching the Wall through Sydney's binoculars.

"Hey, Beth, Kate found some strawberries!" Sydney didn't mean to startle her friend, who swung around, dropping the binoculars on the ground.

"Don't do that to me!" Elizabeth said.

"I'm sorry," Sydney apologized. "But Kate found some strawberries by panel 52W."

Elizabeth picked up the binoculars and handed them to Sydney.

"That's not all I found," Kate said. "A soldier on that panel had the last name Redd. You know what that means, don't you? They've accelerated their plot to Level Red. Anytime now, they could put their plan into action—and we have to find out what it is before someone gets hurt!"

Kate picked her backpack up off the ground and took out her notepad and marker. She printed the words *Hail to the chief at the twilight's last gleaming.* "There's a note with the strawberries, attached to a small American flag. This is what it says," Kate told them.

Elizabeth read the words. "Were the letters all capitalized like you've written them here?" she asked.

"I didn't really pay attention," Kate answered. "But no, I don't think so. I'm almost sure that they weren't all caps."

"Then this note must be from The Professor, or the guy in the suit," Elizabeth decided. "The note that Moose and Rusty left for him was written all in capital letters, the one that said 'Meade me in St. Louis.' "

Kate reached into her backpack and took out a plastic bottle of water. She plopped down on the ground and drank some. "Who do you think The Professor is?" she wondered. "Do you think it's the suit guy?"

"I doubt it," Sydney said, watching the Wall with her binoculars. "At the Lincoln Memorial, Rusty wanted to go and check out *the place*, whatever that meant, and the suit guy said no, that he'd have to talk it over with *him* first. I think *him* might mean The Professor."

"So, we think they might be plotting to do something to President Meade," Kate sighed, "but we don't know who the *him* is or where the place is."

"You've got it," Sydney replied, still watching through her binoculars. "But if your plan works, we'll know soon.

Hey, Elizabeth, isn't that your uncle Dan's friend?"

"Huh?" Elizabeth answered.

"I think I see that Al guy," Sydney went on. "The one who asked me if I was related to President Lincoln. He's over by the center of the Wall."

"Let me see." Elizabeth took the binoculars from Sydney. She focused them until she could see clearly. "Yeah, that's him," she said. "He's just standing there leaning against the Wall." She moved the binoculars away from her uncle's friend and scanned the east part of the Wall and then the west. She saw no sign of Uncle Dan or of the other man who had been with them yesterday morning.

"He's looking all around now," Elizabeth reported, "like he thinks someone might be watching him. There he goes. He's walking along the west part of the wall. Still looking around. Acting sort of nervous."

"I see him," Sydney said. "He's too far away to see what he's up to, though, so keep telling us."

"Who are we looking at?" Kate wondered as she put the water bottle inside her backpack.

Sydney explained, "Yesterday morning Elizabeth's Uncle Dan and two of his friends met us here at the Wall. My Aunt Dee showed them around, and we hung out, too, just to be polite. That man was with us. His name is Al."

Kate was still confused. "Which man? Where?"

"He's walking past 30W now," Elizabeth informed them.

"The guy in the white shirt and khaki cargo shorts," Sydney told Kate. "See, he's almost to where the strawberries are."

"And he's stopping there," Elizabeth reported. "He's looking at the berries. . . . Now he's looking around again. I wonder what he's doing. . . . He's kneeling. Is he praying? No. . . . He's reading the note that's on the flagpole. Hey! He's picking up our package!"

"Oh no!" Sydney cried. "What's he going to do with it?"

"Is he one of the bad guys?" Kate asked in disbelief.

"Now he's lifting the tape on our note. I think he's reading it," Elizabeth continued. "Yeah, he *is* reading it. I knew yesterday that I didn't like something about him."

"He's leaving," Kate observed. "And he seems to be in a hurry. Did he take our box?"

"No, it's still there," replied Elizabeth.

"Let me have the binoculars," Sydney said. She took them from Elizabeth and scanned the Wall from right to left. "Look over there, where the two walls meet. It's Rusty and Moose!"

CHAPTER 6

"We've Got Legs. . ."

"I'll follow your uncle's friend," Kate announced. She stood and grabbed her backpack. "I'll meet you guys at Union Station before my train leaves at two, at that little café on the upper level. If Moose takes our package, send a text message to the Camp Club Girls so they can track him online."

Kate ran off to follow the guy named Al.

Sydney watched Moose and Rusty through her binoculars. The two men walked slowly, looking at all the items that visitors had left to honor the fallen soldiers. They worked their way, panel by panel, along the west part of the Wall, obviously looking for a clue.

"They're getting closer," Sydney reported to Elizabeth. "I don't think they've seen the berries yet. . . . They're almost there. Oh, Rusty sees them! There they go. They're nearly to panel 52W now. Okay, they've stopped."

Elizabeth could see the men in the distance, but she relied on Sydney to tell her what was happening. "What's going on with our package?" she mused.

"Nothing yet," Sydney answered. "It looks like they're reading the names on the panel. At least Rusty is. Moose is bending over. Oh, wouldn't you know it? He's eating one of the strawberries."

Moose had picked out the biggest and best strawberry of the bunch and popped the whole thing into his mouth.

As Moose reached for another berry, Sydney watched his focus land on the brown-paper-wrapped package.

"He's reading our note, Elizabeth!" Sydney watched through the binoculars. "He's turning sideways now so Rusty can't see what he's doing. Yeah, he's reading it!"

"Can I have a turn, please?" Elizabeth asked.

Reluctantly, Sydney shared her binoculars.

Elizabeth peered at the men through the strong, thick lenses. "Oh, now he's putting the package into the back pocket of his shorts. Yuck! He has the hairiest legs that I've ever seen."

"Elizabeth!" Sydney said.

"Well, he does," Elizabeth confirmed. "Rusty looks upset, and Moose is grinning. He's probably thrilled that the boss gave him such an important job. Moose is picking up another strawberry now. He's giving it to Rusty. Hey! Rusty just hit Moose on the arm. I wish we could hear what they're saying," she added.

"He just hit Moose again," Elizabeth observed. "Just before that, Rusty wrote something on a piece of paper and stuck it on the little flag. Now they're leaving."

"Just like yesterday," Sydney said. "They've left a note for The Professor. We have to go see what it says."

Elizabeth gave the binoculars back to Sydney. "But shouldn't we wait and watch for The Professor to come? I mean, at some point he or the suit guy is going to read it, right?"

"Probably," Sydney answered. "But if The Professor is smart, he won't take that note in broad daylight. If anything, he'll just stroll by, looking like a tourist. He'll take a quick look at it, like anyone else being curious. I think he does his dirty work at night, Elizabeth. That's when the graffiti happened, and no one saw him do it."

"I guess you're right," Elizabeth answered. "I'm going to send a text message to the girls." She took her cell phone out of her pocket and typed: MOOSE HAS PHONE. TRACK HIM! BETH.

Then Elizabeth turned to Sydney and said, "So how do we go over there and look at the note without being seen?"

"Girl! You don't see the forest for the trees," Sydney exclaimed. "Look at that crowd. There are so many tourists that it'll be easy for us to blend in. We'll just get in line and go with the flow. Come on!"

The girls walked to the Vietnam Wall and joined the crowd. Surprisingly, though many people gathered there, the noise level was low. The Wall, that morning, reminded Sydney of being in church just before the service began. People talked, but in hushed voices.

As they neared panel 52W, Sydney and Elizabeth heard children laughing. When they got closer, they saw the reason. Two squirrels were busy eating the strawberries. Each squirrel sat with a berry in its tiny front paws and nibbled at it until it was gone. Soon, just one berry was left. Both squirrels lunged for it, but only one got it. The lucky squirrel raced away with the berry in its mouth. It ran across the grassy area toward the trees where the girls had been hiding. Then the second squirrel tore Rusty's note off the little flag. Off it went, in pursuit of the first squirrel, with the precious note in its mouth.

"Oh my goodness!" Elizabeth gasped. Sydney sprinted across the grass, chasing the squirrel. She ran at lightning speed, almost catching up as the squirrel scampered for the trees.

By now, a crowd of people stood watching. Hurriedly, Elizabeth followed Sydney.

"Sydney! Where are you?" Elizabeth was annoyed by

the time she got to the trees.

"Up here," came a voice from overhead. Elizabeth looked up and saw Sydney sitting on a thick lower limb of the tree. Sydney grinned as she waved the note at Elizabeth. "The squirrel dropped it, and I caught it."

Far up in the tree branches, the angry squirrel sat on a branch, shaking its tail and scolding.

"What does the note say?" Elizabeth asked.

Sydney unfolded the paper and read: " 'LIEUTENANT DAN, WE'VE GOT LEGS.' In all capital letters—"

"Girls! What are you up to?" Aunt Dee stood behind Elizabeth, looking very official in her park ranger's uniform.

"Hi, Aunt Dee," Sydney said brightly. "We were just goofing off." She slid down the tree trunk and brushed herself off. "We were in the neighborhood and decided that we'd visit the Wall again. How are things going?"

Aunt Dee stood with her hands on her hips. "Sydney Lincoln, did I just see you chasing a squirrel across the lawn by the Wall? With a whole bunch of people watching you?"

The smile disappeared from Sydney's face. She had no idea that she'd made such a scene. "Yes, ma'am," she answered.

"Girlfriend!" Aunt Dee said. "This is a national

monument where people come to pay their respects. I'm glad that you and Elizabeth want to come here, but it's not a place to play."

As Elizabeth looked beyond Aunt Dee toward the Wall, she saw Moose and Rusty by panel 52W. They were too far away to tell what was going on, but Rusty was holding the little flag and pointing toward the trees. Had they seen Sydney run off after the squirrel?

"We're sorry, Miss Powers," Elizabeth said. "We were just about to leave. Sydney wants to take me to Union Station." She shot Sydney a desperate look. Sydney had no idea why.

"That's a good idea," Aunt Dee said. Her voice was less stern when she spoke to Elizabeth. "I have some tour buses coming soon, so I'll see you girls at supper. Have fun!"

As soon as Aunt Dee left, Elizabeth grabbed Sydney's arm. "Look!" she said, pointing toward the Wall. Rusty and Moose were walking across the grass toward the trees. "I don't think they see us yet. Drop the note on the ground, and let's get out of here."

"Why should I drop the note?" Sydney questioned.

"I'll tell you later!" Elizabeth exclaimed as she tore the paper from Sydney's hand and threw it to the ground. "Run!" she said.

They ran as fast as they could, through the trees and away from the Wall. They ran until they were almost to the Tidal Basin.

"Why did you leave the note behind?" Sydney asked.

"So they'd think the squirrel got it!" Elizabeth dropped to the ground and stretched out on her back, trying to catch her breath. "What if they saw you chasing the squirrel, Syd? At least if they find the note, they might think you never saw it. What if Moose and Rusty were watching the whole time? We could be in big trouble."

Sydney plopped on the grass and sat cross-legged with her head in her hands. "I didn't stop to think," she said. "When that squirrel took off with the note, I just started running. Did other people see me?"

Elizabeth sighed. "I can't believe you just said that. Do you know how fast you can run? Everyone was watching you. You were amazing!"

Sydney looked at Elizabeth. "What if they did see? We're not talking about some common thugs here, Elizabeth. These guys are out to get President Meade."

Elizabeth sat up. "We'll have to be extra careful now," she said. "We'd better get going. Kate's train leaves in an hour."

The girls walked to the bus stop on 15th Street. They watched for Rusty and Moose. Before they paid the fare on the bus and walked to their seats, they looked around to be sure that the men weren't on board. By the time they got to Union Station, they were reasonably sure that they hadn't been followed.

Kate was waiting for them at a café on the upper level of the station. She sat at a small white table with three chairs, sipping a cold soda. Elizabeth and Sydney both noticed that Kate looked serious.

"Hi, you two," she said. "You'd better sit down. I have a lot to tell you."

"We have a lot to tell you, too," Elizabeth replied.

"I'll buy some sodas," Sydney told them. "They don't like it if you sit without buying something."

By the time Sydney returned, Elizabeth had told Kate about the new note that Rusty and Moose left on the little flag and what had happened with Sydney and the squirrel. Sydney placed two Cokes on the table and sat down. "We might be in big trouble," she said.

"Maybe more trouble than you know," Kate responded. "I followed that guy, Al, to a hotel on East Street Northwest."

"That's where the Vietnam Veterans' Reunion is," Elizabeth said. "My uncle is staying there."

"I know," Kate said. "I think I saw him. What does he look like, Elizabeth?"

"Well, he's in a wheelchair. . . ," said Elizabeth.

"A flashy one with lots of chrome," Sydney added.

"He has blond hair, a little on the longish side," Elizabeth continued, "and big muscles on his arms, because he wheels himself around in the chair. He won't use one of those motorized ones. And he usually wears khakis or camouflage, especially when he's with his Vietnam friends. Oh, and I forgot, he has a bushy mustache."

"That was him," Kate said. She took a long drink of her soda. "You're not going to like what I have to tell you."

"What?" Elizabeth said cautiously.

"Well, I followed Al to the hotel. He got on an elevator, and I watched to see what floor he got off on. It was the third. So I ran up the stairs, and by the time I got there, he and your uncle were going into one of the rooms. When they shut the door, I went to the door and listened."

"Kate! Are you out of your mind?" Sydney asked. "What if someone had seen you?"

"I was okay, because the room was next to a broom closet. If I had to, I could have hidden in there," Kate said. "Beth, they were talking about the stuff at the Wall. Al told your uncle about every place that you've been. He knew about the 'Meade me in St. Louis' note and about your going to the Lincoln Memorial and that Sydney listened to those guys behind the pillar. He even knew that you met me at the station this morning, but he doesn't know who I am. And, of course, he knew about the latest note. The one the squirrel got."

Elizabeth said nothing.

Sydney remembered, "At the Lincoln Memorial you thought you were being followed, Elizabeth. I guess it wasn't your imagination. It was your uncle's friend. He's been watching us!"

"I can't believe that," Elizabeth said. "Why would he do that? And why would Uncle Dan let him?"

"There's more," Kate said. "Your uncle said something about talking to a man named Phillips. He said Phillips was watching the situation closely. Then your uncle said, 'If the girls get too involved in this, we might have to—.' I didn't hear the rest because someone around the corner turned on a vacuum cleaner."

Elizabeth spilled her soda, and Sydney hurried to get napkins to wipe it up.

"Beth," Kate said softly, "I think your uncle Dan might be one of the terrorists."

Suspicions

"My uncle is *not* a terrorist!" Elizabeth exploded.

Kate looked at her solemnly and handed her a sheet of folded-up notebook paper. "Stick this in your pocket," she whispered. "Don't lose it, and don't open it until you get back to Sydney's house."

● — ● — ●

By three o'clock, Sydney and Elizabeth were back in Sydney's bedroom. Elizabeth read Kate's note aloud:

> *Elizabeth,*
>
> *I think a tracking device might be hidden in your backpack. That might be how Al knows where you are all the time. From now on, leave your backpack at Sydney's house, but not in your room where a mic could pick up your discussions. Be careful what you say in public, too. Someone might be listening.*
>
> *Kate*

Elizabeth flopped down on her bed as Sydney booted up the computer. "I don't care what anyone says. My uncle is *not* plotting to do something terrible to the president."

Sydney watched the monitor screen turn from black to blue. "You're probably right, Beth, but we have to be careful until we find out what's going on."

"And do you know what else?" Elizabeth continued. "We need to pray. In 1 Timothy the Bible says to pray for those in authority. So we should be praying for President Meade. In Matthew scripture says we should pray for our enemies. We should be praying for Rusty and Moose, the suit guy, and The Professor. And most of all, we should be praying for ourselves that we're doing the right thing."

Sydney clicked on the icon to bring up her e-mail program. "You're right, Beth. We'll form a Camp Club Girls prayer group. If we all join together to trust God, I know He'll help us save the president."

"*If* the president needs saving," Elizabeth reminded her. "We don't know what this is all about yet."

Sydney clicked her mouse a couple of times to bring up a list of new mail messages. Only two waited: one from Bailey and the other from McKenzie. "Elizabeth, even before I agreed with you, you'd decided those guys were terrorists."

"I know," Elizabeth answered, "but now it's getting personal."

Sydney opened Bailey's e-mail.

> *I've been tracking Mr. Green since I got your text message. He went from the Wall a little bit south. Then he turned around and went north. He's been a little northwest of the White House all afternoon. He hasn't moved at all. I hope you guys are okay! Let me know what's happening.*

"I'm going to log on to Kate's tracking site," said Sydney. "My password's Jones, and you're Indiana, right?"

"Right," Elizabeth said. She got up from the bed and walked across the room to sit with Sydney at the desk. Sydney typed the password into the log-in box. Soon a map appeared. A little off from the center of it was a small, glowing green dot. Sydney clicked the zoom icon. The map morphed into a bird's-eye view of Washington, D.C. You could see the tops of trees and buildings as if you were looking down at them from an airplane. All the important streets, highways, buildings, and monuments were labeled.

"This is so neat!" Elizabeth exclaimed. "Kate's outdone herself this time."

"And Bailey's right with her directions," said Sydney. "Moose is northwest of the White House, in Foggy Bottom. From this view, it looks like they're in an apartment house."

Elizabeth remembered that she and Sydney had gotten off the train in Foggy Bottom, but she had no idea that it was northwest of the White House.

"Well, now we know that Moose and Rusty didn't follow us," Sydney said. "According to Bailey's e-mail, they walked from the Wall a little bit south. That must have been when they were coming after us, just before we ran."

Sydney minimized the map screen and brought up her e-mail program. "Then if they turned and went north, they must not have seen that we ran to the Tidal Basin."

Sydney typed her reply to Bailey:

*Great work, Bailey! That area northwest of
the White House is called Foggy Bottom. Keep
watching, OK? In a little while, we'll set up
a schedule so we all can take turns watching
Moose. We're fine. More later. Syd.*

"Did you notice that the blip didn't go anywhere near where my uncle is staying?" Elizabeth asked. "I just know that he's not a part of this."

"You're right, it didn't," Sydney replied. Then she opened McKenzie's e-mail.

Call me online as soon as you get this. Kate has texted me the whole time she's been on the train. She told me everything that's going on. Call me!

Before Sydney could respond, the videophone rang. It was McKenzie. Sydney turned on the Web cam and picked up the call.

McKenzie sat at the computer desk in her bedroom. She wore a pink baseball cap with a picture of a racehorse embroidered on the front. Her orange tomcat, Andrew, lounged on the back of her desk chair.

"We were just going to call you," Sydney said.

"I couldn't wait," McKenzie replied. She twisted a lock of her hair between her thumb and her index finger. "Do you realize what a big deal this is if you've uncovered a plot to assassinate the president? I couldn't believe half the stuff that Kate told me."

"Believe it," Sydney said. "It's all true."

Elizabeth slid her chair closer to Sydney's. "Hi, McKenzie," she offered.

"Hi, Elizabeth," McKenzie answered. "Listen, I've been thinking. That first note you found said 'Meade me

81

in St. Louis, July first," right?"

"Right," Elizabeth confirmed.

"Get off!" Andrew had jumped from the chair onto McKenzie's keyboard. He loved to act up when she was online. "I just Googled the president to find out where he'll be on July first. He's not anywhere near St. Louis. He's going to be in Baltimore. So could you be on the wrong track with all of this?" She picked up Andrew and put him on her lap.

"Your guess is as good as ours," Elizabeth said. "The first of July is Friday. That gives us two days to find out if we're right. If nothing happens by the end of the weekend, I'll have to help out from Amarillo. We're going home on Sunday night. Uncle Dan has a class starting on the fifth."

Sydney picked up a red fine-point marker and scribbled the word *Baltimore* on a scrap of paper. She doodled all around it. Drawing flowers and animals somehow helped her concentrate.

"What kind of class is your uncle taking?" McKenzie asked.

"He's not taking it; he's teaching it," Elizabeth replied.

Sydney penned the words: *Teaching. . .Teacher.*

"My uncle teaches American history at Amarillo Community College," Elizabeth continued.

Sydney scribbled the words: *Teacher. . .College. . . Professor!*

Oh my goodness, she thought. She decided not to say what she was thinking. As Elizabeth and McKenzie talked, Sydney tore the paper into little pieces and tossed it into the trash can under the desk.

"So what's the president doing in Baltimore on Friday?" she asked. She tried hard not to let her feelings show. Inside her brain, a voice shouted, *"Oh no! Kate's right! Elizabeth's uncle is The Professor, the top guy in the plot to kill the president!"*

McKenzie was feeding Andrew now. She held his bowl of food while he sat on the desk and scarfed it down. "He's going to be at Fort McHenry for some Fourth of July weekend concert thing. I can't remember exactly what it's called. Just a minute, I wrote it down." McKenzie set the cat's dish on the desk. The girls heard paper rustling as she looked for the note she'd jotted about the president. "Here it is. It's called a Twilight Tattoo."

Elizabeth gasped.

"What?" McKenzie asked.

"That was Moose's big idea," Elizabeth said. "He made a plan that involved a tattoo, and the suit guy couldn't believe that Moose was bright enough to think of it—"

Sydney interrupted, "Only we thought he meant

tattoo, as in a picture branded on your skin."

"Tattoos aren't *branded* on people," McKenzie corrected her. "You brand cattle."

"Obviously that's not what it means," Elizabeth said. She found a dictionary in Sydney's bookcase. She opened it to the *T* section and searched. "Tattle. . . tattler. . .tattletail. . .*tattoo*! Here it is. Oh, girls, listen to this: 'an outdoor military exercise given by troops as evening entertainment' and 'a call sounded shortly before taps as notice to go to quarters.' It all fits! Taps is a bugle call that's sounded at the end of a day and at military funerals. They plan to assassinate the president at the tattoo!"

McKenzie leaned back in her chair and put her hands on top of her baseball cap. "I can't believe this is happening," she said. "What are you guys going to do? I mean, if you say something and we're wrong, can you imagine all the trouble it will cause?" She took off her hat and set it on the desk. "Just a second, I'm getting an IM from Alexis. She wants to know what's going on—"

"Listen, McKenzie," Sydney said. "We have to go. Will you tell Alexis and the rest of the girls what we just talked about?"

Elizabeth got up and started unpacking her backpack. "Tell her to get a prayer group going, too," she said as she looked through her backpack for anything odd, like a tracking device.

"I heard," McKenzie said. "Will do, and I'll tell the girls to try to figure out more of this. We'll be in touch with you later." McKenzie waved at the camera and signed off.

Elizabeth had everything out of her backpack now. Her camera, a tube of sunscreen, her hot-pink iPod, a pair of socks, lip gloss. . .all of it lay in a pile on her bed. She turned the yellow backpack upside down and gave it a few hard shakes. Nothing fell out. "See," she said. "No tracking device. If anyone is tracking me, it's not with this backpack."

Sydney sat quietly at her desk pretending to straighten papers and organize her bookcase. There was one important clue that she and Elizabeth hadn't discussed, and they couldn't avoid it any longer. "That note we left behind," Sydney said. "The one that said 'Lieutenant Dan, we've got legs.' What do you think it meant, Beth?"

Once again, Elizabeth said nothing.

Sydney felt anger inside of her. She didn't want to be mad at her friend, but something was very different about Elizabeth. She wasn't acting like the same girl Sydney knew from Discovery Lake Camp.

"What's going on with you?" Sydney asked. "Every time I try to talk about your uncle, you clam up. Don't you know you can talk to me if something's bothering you?"

Elizabeth sighed and sat down on the edge of the bed. "My uncle saved his whole company of men in Vietnam by putting himself in the line of fire," she said. "He got shot, and he might never walk again, and, Sydney, that's not right! I get mad at God sometimes because bad things happen to good people. I get mad at my uncle's Vietnam buddies because they can walk and he can't. Then I get mad at myself for feeling that way. I know what kind of a man my uncle is, and now you want me to believe he's a bad guy and is trying to kill the president. Well, he's *not*! I don't know what the note means, but it isn't what you think."

Sydney walked across the room and sat on the bed next to Elizabeth. "I don't want your uncle to be a bad guy, Beth, and he probably isn't. Help me prove that he isn't, okay? I'm on your side. I really mean that."

Elizabeth held the pendant that hung around her neck. It was a habit that helped her to remember the scripture verse engraved on it: *Do not be terrified; do not be discouraged, for the Lord your God will be with you wherever you go.*

"I want your uncle to walk again," Sydney continued, "but sometimes bad things do happen to good people, and you just have to accept that."

As Elizabeth held the pendant, it came off the chain. The pendant remained in her hand, and the chain slipped to the floor. "Oh," she said. "I can't believe that happened. Uncle Dan just took this to the jewelry store the day before we came out here. He had it matched to this nice silver chain." She picked up the chain and checked out the clasp. "That's strange. It doesn't look broken. I guess I must not have fastened it right. Will you do it, please?" Elizabeth held up her long blond hair while Sydney fastened the clasp.

"There," Sydney said. "It's as good as new. And how about us? Are we good as new?"

Elizabeth smiled. "We are," she said softly. "Let's make a pact to prove that my uncle Dan isn't a terrorist. Agreed?"

"Agreed!" Sydney said.

Just then, Sydney's cell phone began to buzz. She took it from her pocket and found a message from Bailey: MR. GREEN IS ON THE MOVE! LOG ON NOW AND WATCH WHERE HE GOES.

Quickly Sydney and Elizabeth logged on to Kate's tracking site. The green blip was moving steadily away from Foggy Bottom. Its rate of speed told the girls that Moose was not traveling on foot. The blip was on New

York Avenue heading northeast out of town. Elizabeth and Sydney sat at the desk and watched for more than an hour as it slowly traveled to the Baltimore-Washington Parkway, on to Maryland 295 North, and along I-95 North. Then it stopped.

"Why is he stopping?" Elizabeth wondered. "Isn't he in the middle of a freeway?"

"Maybe a toll booth or traffic," Sydney answered.

"So now we know he's in a car," Elizabeth added.

"Or a taxi or a bus," Sydney said.

Soon the green blip left I-95 and began weaving through the streets of Baltimore.

"Either he's lost, or he's looking for something," Sydney observed. "It doesn't look like he knows where he's going."

Eventually the green blip traveled east of Baltimore's Inner Harbor and stopped again. The girls waited for about twenty minutes, wondering if the blip would move. It didn't.

"I know that neighborhood," Sydney said. "It's just across the harbor from Fort McHenry. I've been there with my aunt Dee; sometimes she fills in at the fort when a ranger is on vacation. Anyway, that neighborhood where Moose is now was once upon a time a place where pirates hung out."

"Interesting," Elizabeth said. "So now what do we do?"

Sydney was busy typing an e-mail to the Camp Club Girls.

Subject: Camp Club Girls Unite

Moose has moved from Washington, D.C., to Baltimore's Inner Harbor. (Rusty is probably with him.) Let's group chat tonight at 8:30. We need to make a plan to save President Meade, and we have to pray for guidance and safety. Tomorrow Elizabeth and I will go to Baltimore to check out Fort McHenry and to find out more about the Twilight Tattoo. We'll meet you in the chat room.

"We're going to Baltimore?" Elizabeth exclaimed. "How will we get there?"

"That's easy," Sydney answered. "Aunt Dee! The National Park Service has a van that travels from the Wall to Fort McHenry every day. I'll tell Aunt Dee that I want to take you to see the fort, and we can hitch a ride with a ranger. We can spend the whole day in Baltimore sleuthing things out. Plus, we can get into the fort for free."

"What if we run into Moose and Rusty?" Elizabeth asked.

"We won't as long as the girls are tracking them," Sydney replied. "They can let us know if Moose and Rusty are near, and then we can ditch them. Right now, we have other things to think about. The Camp Club Girls need to get organized. We're on a mission to save the president."

On the Move. . .

The girls wasted no time getting to the chat room at 8:30. None of them had much of an appetite at supper that night. Their minds were on how to solve the mystery of Moose, Rusty, and President Meade.

Alexis Howell was the first to "talk." She had been working on the latest clue left by the Wall.

Alexis: *Have any of you seen the movie* Forrest Gump?

> *That note, "Lieutenant Dan, we got legs,"*
> *is like a line from the movie. The line goes:*
> *"Lieutenant Dan,* you *got new legs."*

> *In one part of the movie, Forrest Gump is a*
> *soldier in Vietnam. His platoon gets ambushed*
> *and Forrest saves his wounded officer,*
> *Lieutenant Dan. Afterwards, the lieutenant is*
> *real mad at Forrest.*

Bailey: *Why is he mad at him?*

Alexis: *Because Dan wanted to die in battle as a hero. Instead he lost his legs and was disabled for the rest of his life. He figured he'd be better off dead.*

Elizabeth and Sydney sat at the computer watching the words flash across the screen.

"Some of it is like what happened with my uncle," Elizabeth said to Sydney. "But Uncle Dan never complains that he lost the use of his legs, and I'm sure that he doesn't think he'd have been better off dead. The clue has to have another meaning."

Sydney typed on her keyboard.

Sydney: *Then what happened?*

Alexis: *Forrest and Dan went into shrimping together and got rich. Years later, when Forrest got married, Lt. Dan showed up at the wedding walking. Forrest said, "Lieutenant Dan, you got new legs." The Lt. showed Forrest his new metal legs and said, "Custom-made titanium alloy. It's what they use on the space shuttle."*

McKenzie: *I'm sorry, Elizabeth, but this seems to point right to your uncle Dan. He was wounded in Vietnam and can't use his legs. So Moose and Rusty are using their legs to help him. I bet that's what it means: Lieutenant Dan, we got legs!*

Alexis: *McKenzie, we can't jump to conclusions. Elizabeth's uncle is innocent until he's proven guilty.*

An uncomfortable pause filled the chat room and Sydney's bedroom. Neither Sydney nor Elizabeth said a word. The only sounds were the soft hum of the computer and the gentle patter of rain on the roof.

Bailey: *What's titanium alloy?*

Kate: *It's a metal made of titanium and other chemical elements. It's super-strong, lightweight, and it can withstand high temperatures. The military uses it to make stuff, like planes and weapons.*

The storm was getting stronger. The girls heard the rain falling harder on the roof.

Sydney: *Let's make a plan for tomorrow when Elizabeth and I go to the fort. A storm's coming, and we'll have to shut down the computer soon.*

Kate: *It's been here already. Would you believe Biscuit was outside digging in the pouring rain? He tracked mud all through the house. He's never done that before.*

As the storm raced toward Sydney's neighborhood, the girls made a plan for the next day. Kate told Sydney and Elizabeth how to set up their cell phones to view the tracking site. That way, Sydney and Elizabeth could see where Moose was at any given time.

Bailey and Alexis would be their backup. They'd watch Moose, too, and would report to Kate and McKenzie what was going on. Meanwhile, Kate and McKenzie would dig deeper into the clues to look for any new leads.

Before they signed off, Sydney and Elizabeth promised to stay in touch with the girls by texting them from the fort, and all the girls promised to pray.

Rain poured down on the brick row house. A huge clap of thunder exploded over the house, making the girls jump.

Just then, Elizabeth's cell phone rang. She looked at the caller ID and pressed the answer button.

"Hi, Uncle Dan," she said.

"Hi, honey," her uncle replied. "I'm just checking on you. There's quite a storm outside. Are you girls all right?"

"We're fine," Elizabeth answered. "We were just getting ready for bed. I'm glad Sydney's room doesn't have any windows. I'd rather not see all the lightning."

"So what's on your agenda for tomorrow?" Uncle Dan asked. "Do you and Sydney have something fun planned?"

"We're going to Baltimore to see Fort McHenry," Elizabeth said.

Sydney sat on her bed waving her arms to get Elizabeth's attention. "No!" she whispered. "Don't tell him!"

But the damage was already done.

"I have to go now," Elizabeth said abruptly. "It's probably not a good idea to talk on the phone in a storm. Good night, Uncle Dan."

She ended the call before her uncle could ask anything else about their plans. "I'm sorry. I forgot," Elizabeth said. "Besides, I won't treat my uncle like he's a criminal. Like Alex said, he's innocent until he's proven guilty."

As the wind howled outside, the two girls shared a time of prayer. They asked God to guide them and protect them. They prayed for their friends and family, and especially for President Meade. Elizabeth asked the Lord to do something soon to prove that her uncle Dan was innocent, and she prayed that her uncle might walk again.

Then Sydney and Elizabeth climbed into their beds and said good night.

●—●—●

Sydney awoke the next morning to someone gently shaking her. It was Aunt Dee. The room was dark and quiet, and Elizabeth was still asleep.

"What time is it?" Sydney groaned.

"It's 7:00 a.m.," Aunt Dee answered. "If you girls are going to catch a ride to the fort, you have to get up soon. The power went out for a while overnight, so your alarm clocks are behind."

Elizabeth stirred in her bed across the room. "What's going on?" she asked, sitting up and rubbing her eyes.

"It's time to get up," Sydney told her. "We have to leave in an hour to go with Aunt Dee to the Wall."

The girls got dressed and logged on to Kate's tracking site. The green blip was still in the same spot as the night before, just east of Baltimore's Inner Harbor.

"I'm going to e-mail the girls," Sydney said.

We're leaving in a few minutes to go to the Wall with Aunt Dee. Catching a ride to the fort at 10:00 a.m. Make sure you let us know if Moose moves, in case we're not looking at our phones.

●—●—●

At ten o'clock, Sydney and Elizabeth met Ranger Hank

Ellsworth at the Visitor Center at the Vietnam Memorial. As they rode along in the backseat of his white park service van, Ranger Hank told them about the fort.

"My great-great-great-grandpa fought at Fort McHenry," the ranger said, scratching the short, gray beard on his tan, weathered face. "But you girls probably aren't interested in hearing about that."

He turned the van onto the highway into heavy traffic.

"No, we want to hear," Sydney said. "We want to learn as much as we can about the fort."

The ranger checked his rearview mirror and changed lanes. "Well, when you get there, you'll have to use your imagination," he said. "The story goes like this: Way back in the 1700s, Baltimore was afraid of being attacked by the British. We were at war with Britain. So the people decided to build a fort to protect themselves. They picked a site called Whetstone Point. It was a good place to build a fort, because it was near the city and was surrounded on three sides by water."

"A peninsula," Elizabeth said.

"Right," the ranger agreed. "And it was smart to build the fort on a peninsula, because any ships sailing in to attack Baltimore had to pass it. When they first built the fort, it was just big mounds of dirt. But later a politician named James McHenry raised money for a new and better fort."

A car cut in front of the van, and Ranger Hank maneuvered to another lane. "The people named Fort McHenry after him because he was so generous and also because he was President George Washington's secretary of war."

Sydney took her cell phone out of her pocket and flipped it open.

"The fort is built in the shape of a five-pointed star," Ranger Hank explained. "They did that so each point of the star could be seen from the point on either side. It only took five men to guard the whole thing. One man could watch from each point of the star."

"That was smart," said Sydney. "Then they could see if the enemy was coming by land or by boat."

"Right," said the ranger. "And the new fort was strong. It was made of brick to protect the soldiers who lived inside. When you get there, you'll see how they lived in houses called barracks. There's the Commanding Officer's Quarters, the Junior Officers' Quarters, and two buildings for the enlisted men. That's where my great-something grandpa lived.

"And don't forget to check out the magazine— that's the strong room where the soldiers stored their gunpowder. They added it to the fort during the Civil War to keep ammunition safe from any sparks or explosions. There's a guardhouse on the grounds, too, with some jail cells. That's where they locked up prisoners."

Sydney checked her cell phone, and Elizabeth leaned in toward her to take a look. The green blip hadn't moved.

"Do you know why the fort is so famous?" asked Ranger Hank.

Sydney flipped her phone shut and slipped it into her pocket.

"It's because of 'The Star-Spangled Banner,' " Elizabeth said. "That's where the song was written."

"And the Battle of Baltimore," Ranger Hank added. "That was the one my great-grandpa fought in."

They came to a stretch of highway that was lined with orange barrels and construction cones, slowing traffic even more.

"Sydney, it's a good thing that you didn't live here back then," said Ranger Hank. "If you had, you'd have seen most of Washington, D.C., burned by the British. Thunderstorms, like the ones we had last night, dumped rain and helped to put the fires out. But the White House and the Capitol Building were destroyed.

"After that, the British sailed toward Baltimore.

They planned to take Fort McHenry and then sail into the Baltimore Basin and attack the city. They made it to where Key Bridge is today. From there, they fired on the fort, and that was the start of the battle. My grandpa and the other soldiers were ready for them and put up a brave fight."

Elizabeth was looking out the window, watching the traffic inch along. "That's where Francis Scott Key comes in," she said. "I studied about him. When the Brits attacked Washington, they took an old doctor prisoner. He was being held on a British ship, and his friends worried that he would be hanged. So they asked Francis Scott Key for help because he was a lawyer. He and another guy were allowed to get on the enemy ship and make a deal with them to release the doctor."

"A dangerous proposition," inserted Ranger Hank. The traffic was thinning, and he increased the van's speed. "The British agreed to release the doctor, but not until the battle was over. They figured that Key and his friends knew about their battle plans, so they were stuck on a ship that was shooting bombs at Fort McHenry."

He turned the van onto I-95 North and headed into Baltimore.

"So how does 'The Star-Spangled Banner' fit in?" Sydney asked.

"Well, there was a huge battle," said Hank. "For twenty-five hours the British attacked Fort McHenry. They used bombs that weighed two hundred pounds and had lighted fuses that made them explode when they reached their targets. The Brits used cannons on their ships and fired fifteen hundred bombs at the fort. All the while, Francis Scott Key was on the enemy's ship watching Fort McHenry under attack."

"Key was a religious man," Elizabeth said, "so he was probably praying as the bombs flew through the air. He was a writer, too, so while he watched, he wrote a poem about what he saw. He didn't know what was going on at Fort McHenry, because it was all smoky from the bombs. But when the smoke cleared over the fort, the big American flag was still there. Baltimore had won the battle."

"If they hadn't won," said Ranger Hank, "Key would have seen the British flag flying over the fort instead."

They turned off of I-95 onto Exit 55. The fort was only a couple of miles away now.

"And that poem that he wrote," said Hank, "was 'The Star-Spangled Banner.' "

The Ranger picked up the yellow ranger hat on the seat next to him and put it on his head. Then he entertained the girls by singing:

*"Oh, say, can you see, by the
    dawn's early light,
What so proudly we hail'd at the
    twilight's last gleaming?
Whose broad stripes and bright
    stars, thro' the perilous fight,
O'er the ramparts we watch'd,
    were so gallantly streaming?
And the rocket's red glare, the
    bombs bursting in air
Gave proof thro' the night that
    our flag was still there.
Oh, say, does that Star-Spangled
    Banner yet wave
O'er the land of the free and the
    home of the brave?"*

Just as he finished the song, they turned left onto Fort Avenue. As they drove down the road, soon the girls saw Fort McHenry and the huge American flag towering over it, blowing in the wind. Ranger Hank drove the van to the Visitor Center.

"Here we are, girls," he said. "Come inside and I'll set you up with free passes. They'll get you in here today and for the next seven days, if you want to come back."

"What about the tattoo tomorrow?" Sydney asked. "Will the pass get us into that, too?"

"It will," the ranger answered. "Are you coming to the tattoo, then? Probably with your aunt, since she has to work here tomorrow. Lots of us got called in because the president is coming. It'll be special for you girls to see President Meade. Most people never get to see a real, live president."

"And we hope to keep him that way," said Sydney.

Elizabeth elbowed her. "Thanks for the ride," she said. "What time should we meet you back here?"

"Closing time is 4:45," said the ranger. "I'll be here to pick you up."

As the girls walked out of the Visitor Center, they checked their cell phones. The green blip was moving on water!

"Sydney, he's headed this way," Elizabeth said. "What will we do when they get here?"

Sydney grinned at Elizabeth. "We're going to follow them," she said. "I was hoping that this would happen. Following them is the only way we're really going to find out what's going on."

"But it's too dangerous," Elizabeth protested.

"We'll be careful," Sydney replied. "We can hide in any of the points of the star, and we'll always know where Moose is. We'll be fine."

As the girls walked toward the entrance to Fort McHenry, their cell phones began to vibrate. It was a text message from Bailey: Mr. Green is on the move. headed right at you. on the water. in a boat? B careful.

CHAPTER 9

Fort McHenry Fiasco

Sydney and Elizabeth walked on the weathered brick pathway into the arched entranceway of Fort McHenry. The short, dark hallway was flanked by vaulted doors.

"This is awesome," Elizabeth said. "These doors are ginormous!"

The hallway opened into the bright sunshine and the fort's grassy parade grounds. Just beyond this grassy area were red brick buildings, the barracks that Ranger Hank had told them about. The barracks were two stories high with red roofs, white balconies, and green shutters on the windows. Red-white-and-blue banners hung from the balconies in honor of the Fourth of July, and actors dressed in costumes wandered the grounds making the fort seem more like 1814 than the twenty-first century.

"I just got an idea," Sydney said. "Follow me."

Elizabeth followed Sydney toward a short, stout lady who was one of the actors. She sat on a wooden bench outside the barracks wearing a floor-length, blood-red dress with a tan bonnet. It seemed like way too much clothing for the hot summer day.

"Good day," the lady said as the girls approached her.

"Good day," Sydney and Elizabeth said in unison.

The woman gave each girl a tour map of the fort. "Is this your first visit to Fort McHenry?" she asked.

"It is," Elizabeth answered.

"Nice dress!" said Sydney enthusiastically. "Do you have to get dressed like that at home, or do you change into your costumes here?"

The woman smiled and said, "Oh my! We don't dress like this at home. All our volunteers change here at the fort."

"Neat!" Sydney said. "Elizabeth and I took drama classes at summer camp."

Elizabeth smiled and nodded.

"We had a big room where we stored all the costumes," Sydney continued. "I suppose you do, too?"

"We do," the woman answered. "In that enlisted men's barrack." She pointed to a building across the courtyard. "All kinds of costumes are stored there. You can take a look, if you'd like."

"Oh, that would be great," Sydney said. "Do you think we could try some on, too? My aunt is Deandre Powers, the park ranger. I promise we'll be careful."

The woman thought for a minute. "I know Dee," she replied. "You must be Sydney. She talks about you all the time. Well, I suppose it wouldn't hurt, but make sure you put everything back the way you found it."

"We will," Sydney answered. "Thank you!"

Sydney grabbed Elizabeth's arm and hurried toward the barracks.

"Sydney, what are you up to?" Elizabeth asked.

"We can dress like the volunteers," Sydney answered. "Moose and Rusty will never recognize us, and we can get right up to them and find out what's going on. Then we'll put them back before we go."

The girls opened the door to the enlisted men's barracks and went inside. It was like walking through a time warp into the 1800s. The air smelled musty and cobwebs hung from the rafters. The cobwebs glowed in rays of sunshine that streamed through the only window in the room. It was made up of twenty-five little glass squares, and in front of it sat a small wooden table and chair. An old military jacket hung over the back of the chair, and an inkwell was on the table with some yellowed writing paper and an old oil lamp.

The stuffy room held three rows of simple wooden bunk beds. Each uncomfortable-looking bed had a thin straw mattress and a single flat pillow. Soldiers' shoes hung from several of the bedposts, and muskets stood in their holders, ready for troops to grab them as they hurried out the door. The wooden plank floor creaked as the girls walked on it.

At the back of the barracks was a door marked WARDROBE. Sydney opened it, and the girls found a room filled with racks of costumes: soldiers' uniforms as well as costumes that citizens wore in the early 1800s. The girls went inside and bolted the door behind them.

"So do you want to be a soldier or a lady?" Sydney asked.

"A lady, definitely," said Elizabeth. She picked out an apple green dress and a white bonnet. Sydney helped her pull the dress on over her sleeveless top and shorts. It fit perfectly. Its hem was even long enough to cover the tops of her sandals.

"I'll roast in this!" Elizabeth complained as she pinned her long blond hair on top of her head and tied the bonnet over it. "What will you be?"

"A soldier," Sydney replied. She wiggled into the soldier's uniform—white pants and a dark blue coat with long sleeves and brass buttons. A white sash crisscrossed the front of the jacket, and the jacket's blue and gold collar fit snugly against Sydney's neck. She pulled on a pair of tall black boots. Then she set a blue soldier's hat on top of her cornrows, pulling the visor down just below her eyebrows. "There," she said. "How do I look?"

"Like you're ready for a winter storm," Elizabeth said. "Sydney, you'll be too hot."

"I'll be fine," Sydney argued. "Don't forget to take your cell phone with you. I'll take my binoculars, too. And we should hide my street clothes and our backpacks in here somewhere."

Sydney searched for a place to hide their things.

"Why don't we just hang them up neatly with the costumes?" Elizabeth said. "There are so many clothes in here that no one will notice ours."

"Good idea," Sydney agreed.

The girls made sure that no one was coming. Then they left the barracks through a back door. As soon as they got outside, they checked their phones. The bright green blip was just offshore now, and they saw a string of messages from Bailey and an urgent message from McKenzie: I THINK HE'S ON A WATER TAXI. LOOKS LIKE IT'S LANDING NEAR THE FORT. BE CAREFUL!

"What's a water taxi?" Elizabeth asked, looking prim and proper in her old-time dress.

"It's a tour boat that shuttles visitors around the Baltimore Harbor," Sydney said. "Listen. It says here on the Fort McHenry tour map that each point of the star-shaped fort is called a bastion. We can walk out on the bastions to look all around the fort. It says the big park we saw around the fort is often used for recreational purposes, like hiking, picnicking, and looking out at the harbor. Let's go to the bastion that faces the water taxi dock. Maybe we can see Moose from there."

Elizabeth and Sydney, wearing their costumes, walked onto the long, raised, grassy area that made up one point of the star-shaped fort. The sides of the bastion had strong brick walls, and several old cannons faced outward, reminders of days when soldiers defended the harbor. Sydney took out her binoculars and looked in the direction of the boat landing.

"Perfect timing!" she said. "There they are." She handed the binoculars to Elizabeth.

Moose and Rusty walked toward the fort. Elizabeth noticed that Moose carried a long slender case strapped over his shoulder. "What do you think he's carrying?" she said. "A gun?"

"I don't think they'd be that obvious," Sydney answered. "Watch where they go."

"They're not coming into the fort," Elizabeth reported. "It looks like they're going to hang out in the park instead. They're walking by the water now. . . . They're sitting down on a bench near some trees."

Sydney's cell phone vibrated like crazy. It was another message from Bailey: Percy alert! He's walking around outside of the fort! Watch out!

Sydney sent a reply: We see them. No more text messages until you hear from us. We're going to follow them.

"Let's go," said Sydney. "I want to get close so we can hear what's going on."

"I still don't like the idea of this," Elizabeth said, following Sydney, careful not to trip on the hem of her dress.

The girls walked back to the fort entrance. They went through the brick hallway and then followed a brick path toward the waterfront. They saw Moose and Rusty sitting on the bench. Moose had opened the long slender case and was putting together some sort of contraption. It resembled a weed trimmer.

"What's that?" Sydney asked.

"I don't know," Elizabeth replied. "Let's see what he does with it."

Moose had the thing put together now, and it looked like he was plugging headphones into its handle.

"What in the world is he doing?" Sydney wondered.

Moose got up and put the headphones over his ears. He started walking with the contraption in one hand. He waved it back and forth over the grass while he listened through the headphones.

"I'm calling Kate," Elizabeth said. "She'll know what it is." Elizabeth took out her cell phone, took a picture of the contraption, and transmitted it to Kate. Then she dialed Kate's number. Kate answered on the first ring.

"Are you okay?" she asked. "Bailey said you're following them!"

"We're fine—don't worry," Elizabeth replied. "We need your help."

Since the picture hadn't come out well, Elizabeth described to Kate what Moose was doing with the tool.

"It's a metal detector," Kate told her. "He's waving it over the ground looking for something that's buried there. If the thing detects something metal underground, it gives a signal through the earphones."

When Elizabeth hung up, she told Sydney what Kate said.

"Let's split up," Sydney suggested. "You walk over there, like you're playacting. Say 'good day' to them, and see if you can discover anything."

"I can't do that!" Elizabeth said. "You want me to talk to them?"

"Yes!" said Sydney. "Do it for President Meade."

"You'd better protect me," Elizabeth warned as she walked toward Rusty and Moose.

As she approached the bench, Elizabeth heard Rusty

giving Moose instructions. "Try ten paces east. . . . Now go ten paces north. . . ."

Moose walked along, counting to himself.

Elizabeth walked right up to Rusty. She saw that he was holding some sort of map. "Good day!" she said brightly. She startled Rusty, and he gave a little jump.

"Yeah," he said gruffly.

"Are you enjoying your visit?" Elizabeth asked. She leaned in to get a better look at the map.

"Humph." Rusty grunted, almost ignoring her.

Elizabeth saw a big red X on the map.

"Is there anything you'd like to know about the fort? Anything that I can help you with?" Elizabeth bravely sat on the bench near Rusty to get a closer look at the map. Under the red X was the word *BUM* in all capital letters.

"You can help by leaving me alone, lady," said Rusty.

His steely gray eyes gave Elizabeth the creeps. She got up quickly. "Well, good day, then," she said. But instead of walking back toward Sydney, she circled around the park and met her friend near a grove of trees.

"He's creepier than you could imagine," Elizabeth said.

"So what did you find out?" asked Sydney.

Elizabeth told her all about the map, the red X, and the word *BUM*. Then she texted the other Camp Club

Girls to let them know what was going on.

All afternoon, Sydney and Elizabeth watched as Rusty and Moose wandered around the park with the metal detector. Whatever they looked for didn't seem to be there, or maybe they were even more directionally disabled than Elizabeth. Then, just as the park was about to close, something happened.

Sydney watched through the binoculars. The men were searching back where they'd started, near the bench. Moose stopped by a tree about twenty feet from the shoreline. Rusty hurried to Moose. Then he went back to the bench and picked up his backpack. He took it to where Moose was standing and pulled out a small folding shovel. He knelt down and dug in the dirt beneath the gnarly old tree. After a few minutes, Rusty pulled out a metal box about the size of a box of animal crackers.

"I'm heading over there to see what's going on," Sydney said. "Watch me." She gave the binoculars to Elizabeth.

Sydney walked like a soldier, steadfast and straight, toward Rusty and Moose. She slowed her pace as she neared them. Then she stopped, turned her back to them, and pretended to look across the harbor. Rusty and Moose were so excited about the box that they didn't seem to notice her.

"Handle it real careful, Rusty," Moose was saying.

"We don't need accidents."

Rusty opened the lid of the box and peeked inside. Just then, an enormous explosion rocked the ground and rumbled across the water. Sydney nearly jumped out of her boots.

"What time is it?" Rusty asked Moose.

What time is it? Sydney thought. *Something just exploded inside the fort, and you're wondering what time it is?*

She turned around just long enough to see Rusty close the box and carefully place it in the backpack.

"It's 4:30," Moose said. "When that cannon goes off, it means the fort's closing, doesn't it, Rusty?"

Sydney sighed with relief.

"Yeah," Rusty said, sounding annoyed. "And because you took so long to find this, now we'll have to take it with us."

"But the boss said we should get it done today," Moose protested. "I don't think he wants us hauling that thing all over Baltimore."

"We don't have time," Rusty snarled. "The last boat leaves at five o'clock, and we have to be on it. We'll come back tomorrow. What the boss doesn't know won't hurt him."

Sydney followed behind the men as they walked toward the Visitor Center. They passed Elizabeth on the pathway near the fort's entrance. Sydney saw Elizabeth curtsy. When Sydney caught up to Beth, she told her what was going on.

"The fort closes in fifteen minutes, and we have to return these costumes," Sydney said. "The girls will track Moose. They can tell us where he goes."

The girls scurried back to the wardrobe room and bolted the door. Elizabeth was grateful to get out of the long, heavy dress. Even the stuffy, humid air in the back room felt good against her skin. She hung the dress on a rack and offered to hang up Sydney's uniform while Sydney slipped on her street clothes. Elizabeth was about to return Sydney's cap to a cabinet near the door when she heard a familiar voice.

"Well, here we are, the last stop. A bed for two and nobody sleeps waiting for the alarm," the voice said. "We've been to every room inside the fort."

"Yeah," said an unfamiliar voice. "And the minutes are ticking down."

There was shuffling outside the door. The visitors seemed to be searching for something.

"I can't imagine where they went," said the first voice. "Maybe they've given up spying on our friends."

"Hey, what do you think is in here?" the second voice asked. The doorknob rattled.

"Hide!" Elizabeth whispered. She pulled Sydney toward the racks of clothes.

"No! Out the window!" Sydney exclaimed.

The girls rushed to the only window in the room. Just as they were about to climb out, Elizabeth felt the silver pendant fall from the chain on her neck.

"My pendant!" she gasped.

"Leave it!" said Sydney. "Let's get out of here."

Caught!

The girls barely said a word on the ride home with Ranger Hank. Elizabeth's heart was so heavy that her chest hurt. She was horrified at losing her favorite necklace. But even worse, with a dull ache, Elizabeth had to admit to herself that she knew that first voice they'd heard in the barracks. It was Uncle Dan. And she suspected that Sydney had recognized his voice, too.

When the girls finally returned to Sydney's room, Elizabeth dropped down on the bed and cried.

Sydney booted up the computer and e-mailed the Camp Club Girls. Soon they were all talking in the chat room about the voices near the wardrobe room. The girls agreed that in some way Uncle Dan was involved.

McKenzie: *You know that note you found: "Hail to the chief at the twilight's last gleaming"? "Hail to the Chief" is the song they play when the president shows up. "Twilight's last gleaming"*

*could mean the end of the Twilight Tattoo.
Those words are in "The Star-Spangled Banner,"
too. They plan to kill the president at the end of
the tattoo.*

Sydney doodled on a sheet of paper as she remembered something Aunt Dee had said.

Sydney: *The president isn't scheduled to appear
until just before the fireworks start. There's a
concert and marching presentation at twilight.
When that's over, the president will show up
and make his speech. When he's done, it'll be
dark, and then the fireworks start.*

"In more ways than one," Elizabeth said. She had come to sit next to Sydney at the desk and was reading the words on the screen.

Kate: *I'm almost certain a weapon is in that little
metal box they dug up. Maybe a bomb.*

Sydney scribbled words from "The Star-Spangled Banner" on her paper: *the rocket's red glare. . .the bombs bursting in air. bombs. bomb. BUM!*

119

"Bum!" she said out loud. She grabbed the keyboard.

Sydney: *Elizabeth saw the word BUM on the map near the red X. Maybe it meant bomb. Maybe whoever wrote it couldn't spell.*

Bailey: *So Percy has a bomb in his backpack?*

Sydney: *I think so. And it's your job to keep an eye on him. Let us know the minute he moves.*

Alexis: *I've been thinking about The Professor. I remember a story about Sherlock Holmes, the English detective. His worst enemy was this guy named Professor Moriarty. In the story, the professor was a mastermind criminal. He knew about a secret hiding place for storing bombs during World War II. So maybe our Professor has a secret hiding place inside the fort.*

Sydney: *Maybe you're right. We're going to Fort McHenry with Aunt Dee tomorrow afternoon. She has to work there from five o'clock until the tattoo is done. We won't have much time to find the bomb.*

"Find the bomb?" said Elizabeth. "Oh, Sydney."

"We have to," Sydney said. "Remember, we're not sure any

of this is true. We might be way off track, but if we're not—"

The Camp Club Girls agreed to follow the green blip while Sydney and Elizabeth were at the fort. Only very important text messages would be sent, and those would come through Kate.

●—●—●

The next afternoon, Sydney, Elizabeth, and Aunt Dee arrived at Fort McHenry when it closed, at about a quarter to five. Guests for the tattoo wouldn't be allowed in until six. Aunt Dee gave the girls permission to wander around, but she told them to be back at the Visitor Center by nine o'clock, when President Meade was scheduled to speak.

As they walked through the arched hallway into the fort, the girls took out their cell phones and logged on to Kate's tracking site.

"Moose hasn't moved since they took the water taxi back to the Inner Harbor," Elizabeth observed. "So they probably still have the bomb."

"Not necessarily," Sydney replied. "Maybe Rusty brought it back here overnight; we wouldn't have known if he did."

"I hadn't thought of that," said Elizabeth.

When the girls entered the parade grounds, they saw uniformed troops practicing drills. In the distance they heard drummers and buglers rehearsing for the tattoo.

"Elizabeth," Sydney said. "I think you should call your uncle."

"Why?" Elizabeth asked.

"Because we need to know where he is," Sydney responded. "But don't let on where *we* are."

Reluctantly Elizabeth took out her cell phone and called her uncle's number. It rang several times before Uncle Dan answered.

"Hey, Beth!" he said. "How are you doing?"

"I'm fine, Uncle Dan," Elizabeth said. "Just checking in to see what you're up to. Do you have plans with your friends for tonight?"

Her uncle paused before answering. "We're going fishing," he said. "And where are you going?"

Elizabeth thought quickly. "Oh, we're hanging out with Sydney's aunt Dee."

Sydney put her index finger up to her lips.

"Well, I'm glad to hear that," said Uncle Dan. "Stay close to Aunt Dee tonight, all right?"

What a strange thing to say, Elizabeth thought. "I will," she promised. "I have to go now. I'll talk to you tomorrow." She ended the call.

"So what did he say?" Sydney asked.

"They're going fishing tonight," Elizabeth answered.

Sydney spoke without thinking. "Fishing for President Meade."

As a line of soldiers marched past them wearing 1800s uniforms, Elizabeth said, "I have faith in my uncle, Sydney, almost as much as I have in God."

Sydney didn't say a word.

For the next hour, the girls searched Fort McHenry for the mysterious metal box. First, they checked each of the bastions. As they walked on the ramparts, they looked into the gun barrels of the cannons along the way. They checked the magazines on the bastions—storage areas built into mounds of earth used for stockpiling gunpowder and weapons. Then they moved inside the fort near the barracks and looked underneath the wooden platform that surrounded the enormous flagpole. Above them, they could hear the huge American flag, a replica of the one from the Battle of Baltimore, flapping in the breeze.

Next, the girls went to the barracks, searching each one. Starting on the upper level, they looked under each bed, through every drawer, and inside all the wooden barrels that held supplies. They left no door unopened, and explored every nook and cranny. Nothing!

The last place they checked was the enlisted men's barracks. While Sydney searched, Elizabeth decided to go back to the wardrobe room and look for her pendant.

She found the door bolted shut. Inside, she heard men's voices.

"Look alive, boys!" a man shouted.

"Ready arms. By twos!" shouted another.

As Elizabeth listened, she heard the sound of heavy boots moving toward the door. Quickly she crouched behind some barrels in a corner of the barracks. The door to the room opened and several actors dressed as 1800s soldiers came out. They walked across the wooden floor, past where Elizabeth was hiding, and out the front door.

Elizabeth slipped inside the wardrobe room. Methodically she scanned every square inch of the floor, but found nothing. She also kept her eyes open for the important metal box.

"It's not here."

Elizabeth sucked in her breath and her heart skipped a beat. "Don't scare me like that," she told Sydney.

"The metal box isn't here," Sydney repeated. "I looked everywhere."

"Neither is my pendant," said Elizabeth. "Maybe we should just give up."

"We're not giving up," Sydney protested. "Not until we can prove that nothing evil is going on."

Just then, both girls' cell phones began to vibrate. It

was a message from Kate: MOOSE IS ON THE MOVE. ON THE WATER AGAIN. HEADING FOR THE FORT.

"So what do we do now?" Elizabeth asked.

"We hide outside of the fort and wait," said Sydney. "When they get here, we follow them. Only this time, we have to be careful not to be seen."

Elizabeth and Sydney hid near some trees between the Visitor Center and the fort entrance. Before long, crowds of people arrived. They lined up four or five deep to walk into the fort.

"We'll be lucky to see Moose and Rusty in this crowd," Sydney said. "What if we miss them, Beth? Then what?"

Elizabeth had her cell phone out and was busy watching the tiny screen. "We won't. Not as long as we rely on Kate's Web site. We just have to watch where the green blip goes and keep following it. Even if we can't see them with our own eyes, we'll know where they are."

"And we have to be careful that they don't see us," Sydney added.

The girls watched the blip come onshore. It traveled slowly past the Visitor Center and along the pathway toward the entrance.

"There they are!" said Elizabeth.

Moose and Rusty shuffled along in the middle of the mob. Sydney almost missed them. They looked oddly respectable. Each wore a pair of neat blue jeans and a polo shirt, and Rusty sported a neatly trimmed beard. They blended well with the patriotic crowd.

"Let's go," Sydney said.

Both girls apologized as they cut into the line a few steps behind Rusty and Moose.

"Keep them in sight," Sydney whispered. She fixed her eyes on Rusty's red hair.

The crowd squeezed into the narrow hallway and then swarmed toward the bleachers set up around the parade grounds. Sydney and Elizabeth were pushed along, forced to go with the crowd. When they exited into the fading sunlight, they saw that someone was missing.

"Where's Moose?" Sydney asked.

Elizabeth checked the green blip on her cell phone. "He's still in the hallway," she said.

They found a bench near the barracks and watched Rusty as he sat on a lower tier of the bleachers. They waited for Moose to come out. But he didn't!

"Something's wrong with Kate's Web site," Elizabeth complained. "We've lost Moose."

"I'm going to check out the hallway," Sydney told her. "I'll be right back."

Cautiously Sydney walked to the entrance hall. The crowd had begun to thin out, and Moose was nowhere in sight. She hurried back to Elizabeth. "He's not there," she said. "Tell Kate. Maybe she can fix the Web site."

Elizabeth sent a text message to Kate telling her what was going on.

Everything seems to be working fine, Kate answered. But I'll double check.

"Now what?" Elizabeth asked.

"We wait," Sydney told her. "Keep your eyes on Rusty. Sooner or later, Moose will show up."

"I hope so," said Elizabeth.

The girls watched as the troops marched onto the field. Some soldiers played fifes and others played drums. All marched as if they were going to the battlefield. Swords hung from their belts and some carried muskets.

The troops surrounded the parade grounds and then stood at parade rest. Soon the United States Army Band marched to a stage on the far end of the field. They sat on metal chairs and opened folders of sheet music on their music stands. An announcement boomed over the loudspeaker: "Ladies and gentlemen, please stand for "The Star-Spangled Banner.' "

Then the concert began. Sydney and Elizabeth had no choice but to sit, listen to the music, and watch Rusty. Kate sent several text messages insisting that the Web site was not broken. Still, no sign of Moose.

After about an hour, the sunset faded to dusk, and the

dim crescent moon hung almost overhead.

"Sydney," Elizabeth gasped. "Look!"

Moose came sneaking out of the hallway. He carried the metal box as he prowled close to the fort's brick wall. Just then, Rusty got up and left the bleachers.

The girls' cell phones were vibrating with Kate's message: HE'S ON THE MOVE. EXITING THE HALLWAY NOW.

Elizabeth sent a quick reply: WE SEE HIM.

"You follow Rusty, and I'll take Moose," said Sydney. "I have a feeling we'll end up at the same place."

With their hearts pounding, Sydney and Elizabeth took off.

Quietly and carefully, Sydney stayed close to the fort's wall. She watched Moose slinking from barracks to barracks in the shadow. Finally he paused at an old guardhouse not far from the podium where President Meade was supposed to speak. Sydney saw Elizabeth hiding behind whatever she could find as she followed Rusty. Both girls watched as the men entered the guardhouse, leaving the door open behind them.

The girls met at the open door. Sydney stood on the left and Elizabeth on the right. They could hear the men talking.

"I didn't think you were ever coming out from that secret room," said Rusty. "It's about time!"

"Sorry," Moose answered. "It was dark in there, and I couldn't see my watch. I didn't know what time it was."

"Come on!" Rusty ordered. "That old jail cell is just around the corner. There's a bucket inside where the boss wants us to put it."

Carefully Sydney peeked into the room. The men had disappeared around a corner behind an old jailer's desk. She motioned for Elizabeth to follow her inside. Elizabeth took a deep breath. Then the girls slipped into the guardhouse.

Silently Sydney walked across the room. She peeked around the corner. Straight ahead was a short hallway. At its end was an old jail cell with a heavy iron door. The cell was made of thick brick walls, with no windows. Moose and Rusty were both inside, and Sydney noticed that the cell door had a lock. She watched Rusty take an old tin pail from one corner of the cell, and then Moose gingerly placed the metal box inside.

"We'd better get out of here fast," Moose said.

"I don't think so!" Sydney shouted.

Elizabeth watched with horror as her friend leaped into the hallway and rushed the jail cell. She slammed the door, locking Moose and Rusty inside. Rusty's steely eyes glared at her.

"Who are *you*?" asked Moose.

"I'm your worst enemy," Sydney snapped.

Elizabeth dashed beside her.

"It's those girls from the Wall," Rusty said. "I told you I didn't like something about them." Rusty's voice echoed inside the dark, musty cell. The only other sound came from the tin pail. It was ticking!

"You'd better tell us what you're up to," said Elizabeth. "Or else."

"Or else, what?" Rusty laughed.

In the dim light from the hallway, the girls saw sweat pouring down Moose's face. He stuttered, "There's a b–bomb in here. It's going to g–go off when the f–fireworks start. P–please, let us go. We all g–gotta get out of here." He looked nervously at the pail, inches from his feet.

Through the doorway, the girls heard the loudspeaker announce that President Meade would soon be at the podium.

"You'd better let us go, or we'll all die!" said Rusty. "This is a high-tech military bomb made from titanium alloy. It'll blow this place to smithereens." He took the metal box out of the pail and held it menacingly in front of the girls.

"Run and get help," Sydney told Elizabeth. "Hurry! Go!"

"You come, too!" Elizabeth said.

"*Just go!*" Sydney commanded.

Elizabeth raced out of the short hallway, around the corner, and past the jailer's desk. She bolted out the door and into the darkness. She was almost to the parade grounds when she felt one strong arm wrap around her waist. Then a hand covered her mouth, and someone was dragging her away from the fort and toward the water. The kidnapper pulled her onto a pier and into a small boat. Only then did she get a look at him. It was her uncle's friend Al.

The Rockets' Red Glare

Elizabeth struggled with her kidnapper until she saw Uncle Dan sitting in the boat. Al let her go, and she ran into her uncle's arms.

"I can't believe you're involved in this!" she sobbed. "I always thought you were a good man who loves the Lord."

Uncle Dan hugged her. "I am, and I do," he said. "Now listen to me."

A stranger appeared from the darkness in the back of the boat. He was dressed in black and carried a gun!

"We think there's a plot to assassinate President Meade right here, tonight—and very soon. This is Agent Phillips from the FBI. If you know anything, Elizabeth, tell him right now! It's a matter of life and death. Why were you running, and where is Sydney?"

Elizabeth's heart pounded.

"Sydney has Moose and Rusty locked in a jail cell in the guardhouse." She pointed in the direction from which she'd run. "They have a bomb and it's set to go off when the fireworks start. Sydney told me to run for help. She insisted on staying there to guard them."

Al stood behind Elizabeth and put his hands gently on her shoulders. "See, I knew there was a bomb," he said. "I could sense it from our combat days in Vietnam."

"Tell me exactly what the bomb looks like," Agent Phillips said. "And who are Rusty and Moose?"

"Rusty and Moose work for the boss and The Professor," said Elizabeth. "They're the bad guys. The bomb is in a small metal box that they dug up yesterday afternoon over there." She pointed to the area. "I don't know what's inside the box, but it's ticking, and Moose is nervous. He said if they don't get out of that jail cell, everyone is going to die."

Agent Phillips jumped from the boat onto the dock. He ran as fast as he could toward the guardhouse.

"I'm going, too," Elizabeth demanded. "I have to save Sydney!"

She started to move, but Al and Uncle Dan held her back.

"Let Agent Phillips handle this, Elizabeth," Uncle Dan said. "He knows what he's doing. Sydney will be all right."

Al had one big, strong arm around her shoulder now.

This time, instead of it making her feel terrified, she felt safe.

"I'm sorry, Elizabeth," he said. "I didn't mean to scare you back there. We knew that something was going on, but we weren't sure what it was. If you had screamed, who knows what might have happened. I had to get you to the boat so you'd be safe. I don't know what your uncle would do if he lost you."

Uncle Dan took something from the pocket of his Levi's and held it in his closed fist. "And speaking of losing things," he said, "did you lose this?" He opened his hand and revealed Elizabeth's pendant.

"Oh," Elizabeth gasped. "You found it."

"After you and your friend climbed out the window yesterday," he said. Uncle Dan read the inscription out loud: "'Be strong and courageous. Do not be terrified; do not be discouraged, for the Lord your God will be with you wherever you go. Joshua 1:9.' I gave you this pendant for times like this, Beth. The Lord is with us. He'll save President Meade and your friend. Just you wait and see."

Uncle Dan fastened the chain around Elizabeth's neck. "And by the way," he said. "What were you and Sydney doing in the wardrobe room?"

Elizabeth explained how they had dressed in costume and followed Rusty and Moose. She also told her Uncle about the package Moose was carrying, and she showed them Kate's Web site and the green blip that was inside the jail cell.

— • —

Meanwhile, Agent Phillips rushed into the guardhouse. He passed the old jailer's desk and turned the corner into the shallow hallway. Sydney was standing guard over the prisoners, and Rusty was pleading, "Kid, just go and get the key!"

The FBI agent flashed his badge. "Phillips, FBI!" he said. "Sydney, get out of here. I'll handle this."

Sydney stood straight and tall. "No," she said. "Where's Elizabeth?"

"She's safe," said Agent Phillips. "Get out!"

Sydney didn't move.

"Unlock this door!" Rusty thundered. "We have less than a half hour before this thing blows."

Moose stood next to Rusty, hanging on to the bars. His eyes were glazed, and his face was an odd gray color. "I think I'm going to throw up," he said.

"Sydney, where's the key?" the agent asked calmly.

Sydney felt like she was in an old spy movie, the kind that Alexis was always talking about. "I don't know," she answered.

Agent Phillips stayed calm when he spoke. "We have

to find the key. The only thing that might stop that bomb from going off is to drown it in water. We need to get it out of this jail cell and into the harbor. *Now!*"

Agent Phillips began searching the guardhouse. Sydney helped. They dumped the contents of all the drawers in the jailer's desk and found nothing. They looked in cabinets, under a pile of books, and beneath the mattress of the jailer's cot in the corner. Then Phillips got on his radio and called for help. Within seconds five men wearing black suits burst through the door.

"Oh!" Sydney gasped.

One was the short, dark man she and Elizabeth had seen at the Lincoln Memorial—the boss.

"Arrest that guy!" Sydney cried. "He's the boss!"

The man looked at her as if she were crazy. "Peter Daniels, Secret Service," he said to Agent Phillips.

"Daniels, get President Meade out of here right now!" The FBI agent commanded. "He's in danger."

The Secret Service agent bolted out of the room.

"But you can't let him get away!" Sydney said. "He's the boss!"

Everything was so mixed up. Sydney had no time to tell Agent Phillips the whole story, and he had no idea what she meant. Meanwhile, she watched the boss get away.

"Elizabeth and I were spying on Moose and Rusty," she blurted out. "At the Lincoln Memorial. That guy is the one who was giving them the orders. He's part of the plan to get President Meade!"

Agent Phillips looked at her with disbelief.

"Oh, please, just trust me," said Sydney.

Phillips nodded toward the other men, and two of them ran into the darkness.

"Sydney, I need your help," said Agent Phillips. "Run as fast as you can to the Visitor Center, and see if you can find where they keep the key. Radio the information back to me." He handed her a small walkie-talkie. "Whatever you do, don't come back here. Get as far away from Fort McHenry as you can."

Sydney Lincoln took the walkie-talkie in one hand and started to run. She ran faster than she ever had. Everything was at stake now: the president's life and the lives of everyone in the fort, including her own.

●—●—●

In the Visitor Center, Aunt Dee sat at a desk watching the fort entrance on a security monitor. The entrance was deserted. All of the visitors were in the bleachers waiting for President Meade. Dee looked at a wall clock. It was a few minutes past nine o'clock, and the president was late getting to the podium. The loudspeaker played patriotic music as the visitors waited for him to appear.

Aunt Dee glanced back at the monitor just in time to see Sydney dash through the entrance from the fort. It didn't seem at all odd that she was running. After all, Dee had told her and Elizabeth to be back at the Visitor Center by nine. And they were late.

Sydney ran through the front door.

"Aunt Dee! Aunt Dee! Help!"

Dee jumped up from her desk and hurried to Sydney. "What's the matter?" she demanded. "Did something happen to Elizabeth?"

"Aunt Dee, an FBI agent sent me. There's a bomb in the guardhouse, and we need the key to the jail cell!"

"What?" Aunt Dee asked doubtfully.

Sydney held the walkie-talkie up to her mouth and pushed a button. "Agent Phillips? Please tell my aunt what's going on. I don't think she believes me."

The walkie-talkie crackled. "This is Agent Phillips from the FBI," the voice said. "We have a code red situation in the guardhouse, and we need the key to the jail cell right away!"

"There's a plot to kill the president," Sydney added.

Sydney's aunt rushed into a back room and returned with a big, black skeleton key hanging on a bigger metal ring. "Tell him I've got it," she said.

Sydney tore the key from her aunt's hand and took off.

"Sydney, no!" Aunt Dee shouted. But it was too late. Sydney charged through the darkness grasping the key. As she ran, she remembered the scripture verse on the bracelet Elizabeth had given her: *Be strong and courageous. Do not be terrified; do not be discouraged, for the Lord your God will be with you wherever you go.*

By now, fifteen minutes had passed. A quarter of an hour was all that was left to drown the bomb and get to safety. As the loudspeaker played "Stars and Stripes Forever," Sydney cut across the parade grounds, past the barracks, and into the night. Several Secret Service agents, not knowing who she was or what she was up to, chased her. Sydney was faster than they were. She didn't dare slow down by looking over her shoulder to see if any of them was the boss. Instead, she ran with all her might to the guardhouse.

Sydney slammed through the door. "Here!" she gasped, pushing the key to Agent Phillips.

"Leave her alone!" Phillips ordered the agents who were about to tackle Sydney. Phillips ran to the jail cell with Sydney behind him. "Get out of here!" he told her.

"No!" Sydney exclaimed. "I can help."

Moose was lying on the floor. He had passed out from

fear. Rusty clung to the cell bars, his face ashen. He was no longer the gruff character who talked down to Moose and made demands. Instead, he looked like a frightened boy.

"You'd better say your prayers," Sydney told him as Phillips put the key into the lock.

"I don't know any prayers," Rusty answered.

As Agent Phillips tried to unlock the door, Sydney prayed out loud: "Our Father who art in heaven, hallowed be Thy name. Thy kingdom come. Thy will be done on earth as it is in heaven. Give us this day our daily bread. And forgive us our trespasses as we forgive those who trespass against us. And lead us not into temptation, but deliver us from evil: For thine is the kingdom, and the power, and the glory, forever. Amen."

"Amen," Rusty echoed.

The cell door creaked open, and a team of FBI agents tackled Rusty. Another agent snapped handcuffs onto Moose as he lay unconscious on the cold brick floor. A third agent reached for the metal box with the bomb, but Sydney was faster. She grabbed the box and ran.

"Sydney!" Agent Phillips shouted.

"Let her go," another agent said. "She's faster than any of us. We can't do anything about it now."

●—●—●

On the boat, Elizabeth waited with her uncle and his

friend. In the distance, they could hear "Stars and Stripes Forever" playing on the parade grounds loudspeakers.

"It's almost time for the fireworks to start," Elizabeth said. "I suppose that by now Agent Phillips has canceled them and they've dismantled the bomb. Where in the world is Sydney?"

Uncle Dan smiled weakly. "They'll probably have the fireworks anyway," he said. "It's all done by computer these days."

The two-way radio on the boat started to crackle. Agent Phillips's anxious voice came through: "Dan, Sydney has the bomb, and she's running toward the harbor. As soon as she drops it in the water, get her into the boat and get as far out in the harbor as you can—as fast as you can. Good luck!"

Elizabeth had a sick, sinking feeling in the pit of her stomach.

Al started the engine and untied the boat from the dock. Then a shadowy figure appeared on the crest of the hill near the harbor. It almost flew toward the boat docks.

"There she is!" Elizabeth cried. "She's running to that dock!" She pointed to a boat dock south from where they were. Immediately Al backed the boat out and sped in that direction.

"Run, Sydney! Run!" Elizabeth cried. "We're coming to get you!"

As Sydney ran, clutching the metal box, she prayed that the bomb wouldn't go off. Her heart was pounding when her feet hit the wooden dock. Although it was at most thirty feet long, to Sydney it seemed like a mile. Finally she reached the end of the dock. She dropped the box into the water.

"Swim to us!" Uncle Dan shouted.

Sydney dove in and swam to the boat. Elizabeth helped pull her inside. Then, with Al at the controls, the powerboat sped out into the Baltimore Harbor.

Sydney lay on her back on the boat's floor, wet and gasping for air. "W—we. . .d—did it," she said. "We s—saved P—President Meade."

Elizabeth held her friend's hand. "No, Sydney," she said. "*You* did it."

As the boat sailed a safe distance into the harbor, Elizabeth sent Kate a text message: WE'RE ALL RIGHT. TELL THE OTHER CAMP CLUB GIRLS THAT WE'LL HAVE A LONG STORY TO TELL AROUND OUR CYBER CAMPFIRE.

Kate texted: MOOSE IS ON THE MOVE AGAIN. HE'S HEADING TOWARD THE FORT'S ENTRANCE NOW, REALLY SLOW.

Elizabeth typed back, I KNOW. HE'S IN HANDCUFFS AND SHACKLES.

Kaboom! Pow! Bang! Several explosions thundered across the water making the boat rock.

"Oh no," Sydney said, still lying on the floor. "Did it go off?"

In the following seconds, Elizabeth only saw the stars and the crescent moon in the black sky. Then several bright dots shot into the air over the fort, leaving smoke trails behind them. One exploded into a silver fountain, another into long golden spider legs, and a third showered the fort with sparks of red, white, and blue. "It's only the fireworks starting," she said.

The radio crackled again. "All suspects are in custody," said Agent Phillips. "Percival Malone, Rusty Gates, and also the Secret Service guy Peter Daniels. A fourth suspect is in Washington, D.C., and our agents have him surrounded. Good work, Sydney and Elizabeth. But if you ever do anything this dangerous again, I might have to arrest you!"

Uncle Dan looked at the girls and nodded in agreement. Then they all laughed, happy that the whole thing was behind them.

"Do you think that Agent Phillips will tell us the whole story?" Sydney wondered as she accepted a blanket Uncle Dan found in a seat. "I mean, we still don't know why those guys wanted to kill the president or who The Professor is."

Al settled back in his captain's chair and watched as fireworks spilled over the fort. "I'm sure he'll tell us what he can," he said. "Your uncle and I would like to know the whole story, too."

Sydney sat looking toward the fort. The exploding fireworks cast a strange flickering light on the huge American flag flying near the barracks. Sydney couldn't help but imagine what it was like for Francis Scott Key as he stood on the deck of an enemy ship in the Baltimore Harbor, watching bombs explode over Fort McHenry. She thanked God that tonight's rockets' red glare came from the fireworks.

According to His Plan

The next morning, Elizabeth and Sydney went to the police station to tell everything they knew about Moose, Rusty, and the plot to kill President Meade. Uncle Dan and Al went, too, and Agent Phillips was there to help.

● — ● — ●

Meanwhile, Alexis, Bailey, McKenzie, and Kate were all in the chat room waiting for them to return. The only information they had came from an e-mail that Sydney sent after she and Elizabeth got back from the tattoo. It told everything that had happened at the fort, but there were still lots of missing pieces.

Finally Sydney and Elizabeth logged in.

Bailey: *So tell us what you found out at the police station. And don't leave anything out.*
Alexis: *Yeah. I'm dying to know what happened. I've had "The Star Spangled Banner" playing in my head ever since I read your e-mail.*

Sometimes I hate it that my brain is so musical.

McKenzie: *I didn't see anything about it on the news this morning. Why not?*

Sydney and Elizabeth sat at Sydney's desk. In front of them was an open box of chocolates, a gift from Agent Phillips. Two pieces of candy were missing from the box, and Sydney reached for another. On the shelf near Elizabeth sat a big glass vase filled with two dozen red roses. A white card with gold lettering hung from it, reading: WITH SINCERE GRATITUDE—PRESIDENT WILSON MEADE.

Sydney: *They're keeping the assassination plot quiet. The visitors to the tattoo had no idea that anything was going on, because the FBI didn't want them to panic. It was quicker to get the bomb away from the crowd than to get the crowd away from the bomb. When it was all over, President Meade made his speech as if nothing had happened, and then the tattoo ended with the fireworks.*

Alexis: *So you're not going to be on the news?*

Sydney: *Not unless someone leaks it to the media.*

The FBI hopes it won't happen. They don't want other bad guys to get ideas.

Elizabeth borrowed the keyboard from Sydney.

Elizabeth: *You can't say a word to anyone about what we're going to tell you. This is a Camp Club Girls secret. Let's do a cyber pinkie-promise that we'll take it to our graves.*
Bailey: *I promise.*
Alexis: *And me.*
McKenzie: *I'm in.*
Kate: *Me, too. Biscuit promises, too.*

Sydney and Elizabeth linked their pinkie fingers and promised to keep the secret forever.

McKenzie: *So who was The Professor?*
Kate: *And what was up with the Secret Service guy, the boss?*
Elizabeth: *One thing at a time. We have to start at the beginning, way back in 1967 in Vietnam. The boss—his real name is Peter Daniels—was a soldier then in the United States Army. He was the Dan in the note, "Lieutenant Dan,*

we've got legs," not my uncle.

Alexis: *I'm glad, Elizabeth. None of us wanted*
your uncle to be one of the bad guys.

Elizabeth chose a square piece of chocolate from the box before she continued.

Elizabeth: *Peter Daniels had a twin brother*
named Adam, and they fought together in the
Vietnam War. They were both in a platoon
called White Skull, and they were in the worst
of the fighting.

Sydney took over the keyboard while Elizabeth ate the chewy caramel.

Sydney: *One day, there was a terrible battle.*
The White Skull troopers were under attack,
and they were outnumbered. So their leader,
Sergeant Kuester, told them to retreat. He
figured if he didn't get his men out of there,
they'd all get killed.

McKenzie: *How do you know all this?*

Sydney: *Because Sergeant Kuester is here in D.C.*
at the Vietnam Veterans' Reunion, the same

one Beth's uncle is at. The FBI found out that Sergeant Kuester had been Daniel's platoon leader, and they figured he might have an idea why Daniels wanted to kill the president. It was his information that got Peter Daniels to confess.

Bailey: *So why did he want to kill the president?*

Sydney: *President Meade was in the White Skull platoon, too, when he was a young soldier. When Sgt. Kuester told his men to retreat, Meade froze. Adam Daniels, the boss's twin brother, tried to get Meade out of there, but Meade went crazy. He started fighting with Adam, like he was the enemy or something—*

McKenzie: *It was Agent Orange, wasn't it? I've thought from the beginning that whoever we were looking for was sick from that.*

Sydney: *Sorry, McKenzie, but you were wrong about that. It had nothing to do with Agent Orange. Meade just froze in fear.*

Sydney helped herself to another piece of candy before going on with the story.

Sydney: *Sgt. Kuester realized that two guys were*

149

missing, so he went back to get them. When Peter Daniels found out that one of the missing guys was his brother, he went to help.

Of course, when they got to them, they found Meade fighting with Adam Daniels. Adam was trying to drag Meade out of there while they were under attack. Kuester managed to get between them and wrestle Meade to the ground. But the enemy fired at them. The sergeant got shot in the leg and Adam Daniels fell to the ground—dead. Kuester managed to get out and Peter Daniels rescued Meade, but secretly he blamed Meade for the death of his twin brother.

Sydney pushed the keyboard toward Elizabeth. "You tell the next part," she said.

Elizabeth: *After he got out of the army, Peter Daniels became a police officer in Washington, D.C. He worked his way up to the rank of lieutenant.*

Kate: *And that's why they called him Lieutenant Dan in the note.*

Elizabeth: *Right. Wilson Meade became a*

politician and was elected to the United States Senate. He and Peter Daniels were friendly, but Daniels was just like Jesus' disciple Judas. He pretended to be Meade's friend, but in the end, he betrayed him.

When Meade got elected president, he wanted Peter Daniels as one of his Secret Service guys, because he trusted Daniels with his life. In fact, we found out today that it was Daniels who saved President Meade when he was almost shot at the National Air and Space Museum.

Kate: *So the boss saved Meade's life twice. Once in Vietnam and again at the Spirit of St. Louis thing.*

Elizabeth: *Meanwhile, Daniels was getting angrier that his brother was dead. He hated it that Meade was not only alive, but had also become the president of the United States. He just couldn't get it out of his head that Meade was responsible for Adam's death.*

McKenzie: *So he decided to get even.*

Elizabeth wiped her chocolaty fingers on a piece of scrap paper.

Bailey: *What about The Professor?*
Alexis: *And how do Moose and Rusty fit into all this?*

Sydney asked Elizabeth to go down to the kitchen to get some bottles of water. They needed something to wash down the chocolates. In the meantime, she went on with the story.

Sydney: *Daniels knew a scientist who had helped create the space shuttle. He was a troublemaker and hated the government, so he got kicked out of NASA. Daniels figured he'd be more than willing to help get rid of Meade, so he got Professor Hopkins to create a miniature smart bomb made of titanium. It was tiny enough to fit into that little metal box Moose and Rusty had, but powerful enough to destroy all of Fort McHenry and most of the peninsula it's built on.*
Alexis: *So Hopkins was the mastermind professor, like Professor Moriarty in the Sherlock Holmes stories.*

Elizabeth returned with two bottles of water. Sydney

opened hers and took a drink.

> Sydney: *The Professor was the brains behind it all. Plus, he knew his way around the fort, so he decided where the best place was to plant the bomb. When they arrested him last night, he confessed to his part in the plot, but he blamed it all on Daniels.*

> Bailey: *And what about Moose and Rusty?*

Sydney gave the keyboard to Elizabeth.

> Elizabeth: *Daniels and The Professor turned out to be cowards. They didn't want to get killed if the bomb went off too soon, and they didn't want to be connected with the assassination, so they got Moose and Rusty to do their dirty work.*

> *Moose and Rusty were both in trouble for not paying their taxes, and Daniels promised they wouldn't go to prison if they helped him plant the bomb. As much as possible, Daniels tried to stay out of it. That's why he left those messages at the Wall. He didn't want to be seen with Rusty and Moose.*

Kate: *So did Moose and Rusty confess?*

Elizabeth: *They sure did. They told the FBI a lot of stuff. They said since Daniels was a Secret Service agent, he was allowed at Fort McHenry to bury the box with the bomb. He told the park ranger he was checking the place ahead of the president's visit.*

McKenzie: *Then he's the one who made the treasure map.*

Elizabeth: *He made the map. But Rusty and Moose messed up. They were supposed to plant the bomb that afternoon. The Professor wanted them to put it in a secret room in the fort's hallway, the one that Moose hid in last night. But Daniels wanted it closer to where President Meade was supposed to give his speech. He told Moose and Rusty to hide it in the jail cell. It was all supposed to be done the day before the tattoo. But it got too late and Moose and Rusty took the bomb with them. They weren't supposed to be anywhere near the fort on the night of the tattoo. Kate, if not for your tracking device, last night would have been a disaster.*

McKenzie: *What did your uncle say, Elizabeth?*

Kate: *And what about his friend Al? Was he*
following you?

Elizabeth took a drink from her bottle of water.

Elizabeth: *That first day at the Wall, when I*
found the "Meade me in St. Louis" note, my
uncle was suspicious. When I didn't want to
go to lunch, he figured something was going
on. He was worried because I'd told him
about our sleuthing at camp. So he asked his
friend Al to keep an eye on me for a while. He
was afraid I wouldn't be safe in the city.

Kate: *Was I right that they put a GPS in your*
backpack?

Elizabeth: *No. There was no tracking device. But Al*
soon figured out that we were on to something.
He was reading those notes at the Wall, too.
None of them made sense to him and Uncle
Dan, but they figured out, like we did, that
something was going on with President Meade.

Elizabeth helped herself to one more piece of candy.

Elizabeth: *Uncle Dan called Agent Phillips from*
the FBI. Phillips was Uncle Dan's old army

buddy. My uncle told Phillips about the notes at the Wall and also the two suspicious-looking guys who left them there.

Kate: *So that's what I heard when I was listening outside their hotel room that day.*

Elizabeth: *Right. Phillips wasn't sure what was going on, but decided that by following us they would keep us safe, and maybe find out what, if anything, we knew. I'd accidentally told my uncle we planned to go to Fort McHenry, so he, Al, and Agent Phillips followed us. But they lost us when we changed into costumes. They saw us go into the enlisted men's barracks but didn't see us come out. When I heard them outside the door to the wardrobe room, it sounded like they were looking for something. Turns out that they were looking for us!*

She pushed the keyboard over to Sydney's side of the desk and asked her to finish the story.

Sydney: *By the time Uncle Dan found Elizabeth's pendant, we had already left the fort. Agent Phillips figured we'd gone out the window.*

*So Al went looking for us, and guess what he
found instead—Rusty's map. He must have
dropped it on his way to the water taxi. And
guess what it was written on—the back of a
flyer announcing the Twilight Tattoo. So that's
how Uncle Dan and his friends found out
that maybe something was going to happen
at the tattoo. Then when they found out that
we were there last night, they were doubly
suspicious.*

Alexis: *It's a good thing they followed you last
night. You both might have been killed.*

Sydney: *I don't think so. I think we'd have found
a way to save the president. I don't know how,
but the Lord would have helped us.*

Alexis: *He did help you! It all worked out
according to His plan. By the way, what does
your mom think about all of this?*

Sydney put the lid on the box of candy. She and
Elizabeth had decided to save some for later.

Sydney: *Mom didn't know anything about it until
we got home last night. Aunt Dee brought us
here in one of the ranger's vans. Uncle Dan*

and Al came along and explained the whole thing to my mom. At first she was mad. But then she understood that we saved President Meade's life. She cried and hugged us because we were safe. Then I couldn't believe my ears. She said kids like us made the world a better place!

McKenzie: *All right! Let's hear it for the Camp Club Girls!*

A soft knock sounded on Sydney's bedroom door and her mom peeked inside. "I'm sorry to interrupt," she said, "but I just invited Elizabeth's uncle and his friend over for some barbeque. Dee's starting the grill. Would you girls come help us get ready, please?"

"Sure, Mom," Sydney answered. "We'll be down as soon as we've said good-bye to our friends."

Sydney's mom smiled and closed the door.

Elizabeth: *We have to go. Uncle Dan and Al are coming over for a cookout.*

Bailey: *Have a safe trip home.*

McKenzie: *We'll keep praying that your uncle Dan will walk again real soon.*

Elizabeth: *Do you know what? I'm not angry about*

that anymore. This whole adventure taught me that Psalm 37:8 is true: "Refrain from anger and turn from wrath; do not fret—it leads only to evil."

If you enjoyed

SYDNEY'S D.C. DISCOVERY

be sure to read other

CAMP CLUB GIRLS

books from BARBOUR PUBLISHING

Book 1: Mystery at Discovery Lake
ISBN 978-1-60260-267-0

Book 3: McKenzie's
Montana Mystery
ISBN 978-1-60260-269-4

Book 4: Alexis and the
Sacramento Surprise
ISBN 978-1-60260-270-0

Book 5: Kate's Philadelphia Frenzy
ISBN 978-1-60260-271-7

Book 6: Bailey's Peoria Problem
ISBN 978-1-60260-272-4

AVAILABLE WHEREVER BOOKS ARE SOLD.